P9-CLX-685

Runt

Also by V. M. Caldwell

The Ocean Within
Tides

Runt

THE SOUTH LIBRARY

V. M. Caldwell

MILKWEED EDITIONS

The characters and events in this book are fictitious. Any similarity to real persons, living or dead, is coincidental and not intended by the author.

© 2006, Text by V. M. Caldwell
All rights reserved. Except for brief quotations in critical articles or reviews, no part of this book may be reproduced in any manner without prior written permission from the publisher: Milkweed Editions, 1011 Washington Avenue South, Suite 300, Minneapolis, Minnesota 55415.
(800) 520-6455
www.milkweed.org

Published 2006 by Milkweed Editions
Printed in Canada
Cover design by Brad Norr Design
Cover photo: Corbis
Interior design by Dorie McClelland
The text of this book is set in Adobe Garamond Pro.
06 07 08 09 10   5 4 3 2 1
First Edition

Milkweed Editions, a nonprofit publisher, gratefully acknowledges sustaining support from Emilie and Henry Buchwald; Bush Foundation; Patrick and Aimee Butler Family Foundation; Cargill Value Investment; Timothy and Tara Clark Family Charitable Fund; Dougherty Family Foundation; Ecolab Foundation; General Mills Foundation; Greystone Foundation; Institute for Scholarship in the Liberal Arts, College of Arts and Sciences, University of Notre Dame; Constance B. Kunin; Marshall Field's Gives; McKnight Foundation; a grant from the Minnesota State Arts Board, through an appropriation by the Minnesota State Legislature, a grant from the National Endowment for the Arts, and private funders; an award from the National Endowment for the Arts, which believes that a great nation deserves great art; Navarre Corporation; Debbie Reynolds; St. Paul Travelers Foundation; Ellen and Sheldon Sturgis; Target Foundation; Gertrude Sexton Thompson Charitable Trust (George R. A. Johnson, Trustee); James R. Thorpe Foundation; Toro Foundation; Serene and Christopher Warren; W. M. Foundation; and Xcel Energy Foundation.

Library of Congress Cataloging-in-Publication Data
Caldwell, V. M., 1956-
  Runt / V.M. Caldwell.— 1st ed.
    p. cm.
  Summary: Although he tries to make a home with his older sister and her boyfriend after his mother's death, twelve-year-old Runt feels like an outsider until a young cancer patient and his family show him how life can become more meaningful.
  ISBN-13: 978-1-57131-662-2 (hardcover : alk. paper)
  ISBN-13: 978-1-57131-661-5 (pbk. : alk. paper)
  ISBN-10: 1-57131-662-0 (hardcover : alk. paper)
  ISBN-10: 1-57131-661-2 (pbk. : alk. paper)
  [1. Cancer—Fiction. 2. Conduct of life—Fiction. 3. Brothers and sisters—Fiction.] I. Title.
  PZ7.C127435Run 2006
  [Fic]—dc22

                                    2005027358

This book is printed on acid-free paper.

To all the real-life Remicks and Currans

Deepest thanks to:

Maggie
Frenchs Forest, New South Wales, Australia
for friendship, insights,
and benign harassment to finish the manuscript

Catherine
Great Barrington, Massachusetts
for sympathy, empathy,
and the concept of "gaining on it"

and to

Rosemary
Buffalo, New York
for unfailing moral support
throughout the six years
it took to write and revise this story.

Runt

1

"Runt?"

The whisper hovered above him and then moved beyond his reach.

"Runt?" Someone patted his shoulder. "I'm going to work."

He pulled the blanket tighter. Was he dreaming?

"Cole's asleep. Don't wake him, now."

Whose voice was that? He *ought* to know . . .

"Eat whatever you like. Just clean up after, all right?"

Runt forced his eyes open. Gray light came through plastic blinds and cast a faint shimmer onto the brown darkness around him.

"I'll be home by four thirty."

Runt blinked and pushed himself onto one elbow. His sister was wearing a turquoise uniform, a striped apron, and a nametag. Behind her, the clock on the microwave glowed 5:43.

"Be good."

Runt managed a small nod. Helen gave him a quick smile and tiptoed to the door. A sliver of light winked into the trailer and vanished as quickly as it had appeared.

Runt dropped back onto his pillow. He wasn't at home. He wasn't even in Farnham anymore. He was in a trailer, near some place called Westfield, and the sister he hadn't seen in six years had just left for work . . .

Runt wrenched himself upright. Helen was gone! He was alone in the trailer with Cole. Alone with a stranger.

His heart pounded. He had no idea where his sister worked or how to reach her. The air smelled stale and the walls seemed to be closing in. He slipped from beneath the blanket and shot a quick glance to his right. A foldout double bed nearly filled the far end of the trailer. A crest of black hair was visible above the sheet. Runt crept to the outside door and slipped through it. The click as it closed sounded to him like a cannon.

Cole's small black truck was where Helen had parked it last night. Had she walked to work, or was there a bus stop nearby?

The early May dawn was damp, and he shivered. Why hadn't he thought to grab his jacket? He shrugged. At least he'd had the sense to sleep fully-clothed. Silently, he went down the steps. Beneath the thin soles of his sneakers, the ground was hard and cold.

To his left lay the trailers they had passed last night. A bank of thorny looking bushes as tall as the trailers and covered with small oval leaves stood across from him. To his right were more trailers, each topped with a small satellite dish. Just beyond the third one, the road turned sharply and disappeared. He'd see what lay in that direction.

Ten minutes later, the road curved again and came to an end. A dozen trailers filled half a clearing. In front of them were five pickup trucks, two motorcycles, and the remains of a rusted-out car. Plastic toys were scattered among litter and clumps of grass.

At one edge of the clearing, a dumpster overflowed with trash. Behind it, there appeared to be a path through the trees.

Wondering why one end of the park was so different from the other, Runt walked around the dumpster and into the woods.

Branches began to take on colors as the sky lightened: muted gray-greens, olives, and dark browns. Runt slipped into his slow-moving state, drawing comfort from the trees and bushes that were like the ones back home. One part of him knew that he'd been away from Farnham for less than a day, but the rest of him felt as though he'd been gone half a lifetime.

After his mother's funeral yesterday, his aunts had claimed his sisters—Laura, Mary, and Eve. His mind wandered back to their youngest siblings, Mercy and Hope, whose burials they hadn't been allowed to attend . . .

Late last night they'd pulled up in front of the trailer and Helen had shown him the low bench in the kitchen that was to be his bed. Cole had been out on business—he worked nights, Helen said—and Runt had waited long into the night for any sound of this stranger . . .

Runt stumbled, caught himself, and swore. He'd better keep his mind on what his feet were doing. The trail became rocky and abruptly grew steeper. At the top of the rise, it fell away to a sharp slope. A hundred yards from the bottom of the hill stood an iron fence. Beyond it lay neatly trimmed grass veiled with dew. Headstones of shiny black and dull brown, of deep pink and dark gray, stood among curving paths. Here and there, brightly colored flowers sprouted from urns. This cemetery wasn't remotely like the one in Farnham—it was quietly stunning, ordered yet graceful, and exuded a serenity that beckoned him to be part of it.

Getting down there wasn't going to be easy . . .

He searched among the trees until he spotted a sturdy looking sapling. He retied his sneakers, wished himself luck, and plunged forward, one arm protecting his face, the other reaching for the slender tree trunk. He jerked to a stop, his left foot found a rock, and he slowly righted himself. He caught his breath and looked for another sapling that would bear his weight. A dozen tree-to-tree lurches later, his feet slid out from under him. Bumping across rocks, sticks, and roots, and finally *through* a rotting log, he tumbled his way to the bottom.

He lay still for a moment, praying that nothing was broken. He blinked several times and discovered that his left eye ached and his vision was blurred. He raised a hand to investigate and a sharp pain stabbed his left shoulder. He transferred his weight to his right hand and cautiously extended his arm. Nothing shifted or clicked the way it had that time he'd broken his ankle. He eased himself into a sitting position and tested his other joints. He'd torn his shirt and he was covered in scrapes, but he'd live.

A burst of twittering erupted above him. Several birds perched among branches that were still mostly bare. Was that little one a wood thrush? It sang briefly. Yes, it was! And the other little bird, the one chattering and scolding, was a wren. He was pretty sure the third bird was some kind of swallow.

The wren suddenly launched herself from her perch, leaving the slender branch bouncing behind her. She flew to the fence, paused to tip her head, and took off again. Groaning softly, Runt got to his feet.

The black iron fence was freshly painted and eight feet high. The railings that held the spokes upright looked pretty sturdy, but he'd banged himself up enough for one day. He'd follow the fence until he came to a gate.

Five minutes later, he found one. His heart leapt and then fell. The gate was tightly secured with a padlock. There was a sign above it.

WESTFIELD CEMETERY & GARDENS

GATES OPEN 10 AM TO 4 PM, NOVEMBER–APRIL

8 AM TO 6 PM, MAY–OCTOBER

Runt sighed. It couldn't be *too* much longer until eight o'clock, could it? He frowned at his empty left wrist. He hadn't regretted selling his watch—not since Christmas morning, when Mary and Eve's smiles had lit up the Remicks' otherwise empty front room—but it was darned inconvenient never knowing the time.

He peered through the fence. To his left, a brick cube without windows bore the international signs for "Men" and "Women." Had they locked the gates to keep people out of the restrooms? That didn't make sense. Maybe there was something worth stealing in that other building, the large stone one to his right.

He shrugged. Someone would come, eventually. And whoever it turned out to be didn't need to know that he'd been waiting. He climbed part way up the hill and hunched down behind a large maple tree. The air around him grew steadily heavier, and he slipped into sleep.

He awakened midday feeling queasy and sore. Cautiously, he made his way back to the gate. It was open, and no one was in sight. He chose a path that led away from the stone building. He'd get an overview first and explore more thoroughly later.

He walked slowly, letting his eyes wander. The cemetery back home hadn't had bushes or flowers, just grass and a few diseased elms. There were all kinds of trees here. Most were just starting to bud, but some of the smaller ones were covered with flowers. One with pale purple blossoms looked a bit like a willow, with branches that almost touched the ground. Another tree had red-and-white flowers shaped like tulips. The grass beneath it was littered with petals; it must have been among the first to bloom.

He followed path after path, randomly wandering left or right, and paused at a drinking fountain. The water stayed cold all the way to his empty stomach. The width of a shiny black headstone caught his eye, and he crossed the grass to read it:

KNOCHENHAUER.

He wrinkled his nose. How would a person pronounce that?

"Hey, kid!"

Runt turned and leapt sideways in the same move.

"How come you're not in school?"

2

Runt took several steps backward. In front of him was a wheelchair. It was occupied by someone about his height, but considerably larger in size. It was difficult to tell the person's age, or even its gender. A pale, puffy face was crowned by bright orange hair—all wispy and thin, like a baby's. There were deep circles under eyes without lashes.

"Don't you know you get *stupid* if you cut school?" A wide grin appeared. "Or don't you care about getting stupid?"

Runt's heart staggered toward its natural rhythm.

"Nice shiner, kid!"

Runt brought his left hand half way to his eye before letting it fall.

"You must be pretty scrappy. You got a name?" The grin reappeared. "Or did the guy you were fighting take it off you?"

Runt's face burned. "I've got a name," he stammered. "But no reason to tell you."

"Suit yourself, kid." The person shrugged. "Mine's Mitch, but Noah . . ." He pointed to an elderly, spade-carrying man some distance away. ". . . calls me Sport."

Runt scowled at the ground. Who cared what his name was? Why was he *here,* spoiling the afternoon? And how had he sneaked up so quietly?

"Made you jump, didn't I?" Mitch chuckled. "But if I said I was sorry, I'd be lying!"

Runt's cheeks grew warm again. "You get kicks out of giving people heart failure?"

"I knew you wouldn't keel over," Mitch retorted. "You may be skinny, but you look healthy enough. If you can't take a joke . . ."

"I can take a joke." Runt's eyes narrowed. Why was he even talking to this kid?

"Good!" Mitch grinned again. "I'm full of tricks!"

Runt turned away and began to walk quickly.

"Hey, kid!" Mitch called after him. "See you around!"

Runt dug his toes deep and began to run. Not if he could help it!

He galloped past half an acre of headstones and plantings without seeing them. Only when he reached the fence on the far side of the cemetery did he stop and look back. The wheelchair was nowhere in sight, but he spied the man with the spade again.

"Sport?" Runt snorted. The kid couldn't even walk, for Pete's sake. He couldn't be very athletic. And scaring people wasn't exactly being a sport. But he didn't have to sneak up on a guy to spook him—just *looking* at him was scary. That puffed-up face, and that weird orange hair . . . Runt scowled. And where'd he get off asking all those questions?

Runt shoved the wheelchair and its occupant from his mind and studied his surroundings. There were more shade trees in this part of the cemetery: wide maples and old oaks and tall sycamores. Most of the headstones were on the small side, and all of them were gray. He was in the process of deciding he liked the way they looked when a drop of rain splashed his cheek.

The clouds above him were muddy looking and moving

quickly. He looked at the fence and his shoulders fell. He had no idea where he was in relation to the hill he'd come down—and climbing that hill was the only way he knew to get back to the trailer. He had no choice but to go back to the main gate.

He sighed crossly. He'd go slowly, that was all, and hope the kid in the wheelchair had left.

Five minutes later, the heavens opened up. By the time Runt reached the gate, he was shivering from head to toe. He ducked around to his left and hurried along the fence as it curved toward and away from the hill. Apprehension clutched his insides. Where had he come down? He squinted at the slope. Was there a break in the trees at the top? Was that the path? He searched the brush above him, spied the remains of the log he'd demolished in his slide down, and yelped with relief. This was it!

He looked at the landmarks around him, fixed them firmly in his mind, and started up. Water washed past him in icy little streams. His feet slid downward and his fingers burned as they struggled to grasp slippery branches. He fell several times, and sparks appeared in front of his eyes when his chin struck a root. Two-thirds of the way to the top, breathing hard, he leaned against an ash tree to rest. The metallic taste of the rain mingled with the salty bitterness of his sweat. He felt, rather than heard, his stomach growl.

"Quiet!" he scolded. "I can't deal with you now!"

His stomach complied. He took a deep breath and pushed himself away from the tree. "This hill ain't going to help you," he muttered. "So look sharp."

By keeping his mind on the job, Runt managed to come within ten feet of the path. But in the crest at the top of the ridge, he met his match. Most of the roots were too short to grasp, and those that were longer were easily broken. Runt slid backward and down a dozen times before tears of frustration stung his eyes.

"You've *got* a brain, Runt. Use it!"

As his stomach had done, his brain complied. Almost immediately, his eyes picked out a diagonal route to the top. It would take him thirty yards farther along the ridge, but there were saplings he could use as handholds the whole way.

By the time he reached the dumpster, it was dusk. The rain had eased to a drizzle and he paused to look at his torn and swollen hands. The cemetery would be his haven, his sanctuary, but he'd sure have to find a better way to get there.

As he walked, a chant began in his mind: *Please be there, please be back from work, please be there . . .*

He'd barely begun to know his sister again, but he sure didn't want to have to meet Cole Martin—until yesterday, he hadn't even known the man *existed*—without Helen.

Runt came to a halt at the steps to No. 17. A light was on at the far end of the trailer. Helen, or Cole? His stomach muscles tightened. Where else could he go? *No* place, that's where . . .

He climbed the first step and stopped. This was where he lived now, but he couldn't just barge in. He climbed again, knocked twice, and winced. Lord, his hands hurt!

There was a sharp *snap!* in the kitchen and Runt's heart pounded harder. Someone had closed a cupboard door . . .

But *who?*

3

The aluminum door flew open and a clean-shaven man looked down at him with piercing dark eyes. Muscles bulged beneath his maroon T-shirt. His wavy black hair was meticulously combed and something glinted in the lobe of one ear.

"I'm . . ." Runt stammered. "I'm . . ."

The man raised an eyebrow. "You're *what?*"

"Helen's brother."

The man suddenly laughed, revealing a set of square, even teeth. "Hey, Helen!" he called over his shoulder. "Come see what the cat dragged in!"

"Runt?" Helen called anxiously. "Is he here, Cole?"

The man had seemed to fill the doorway, and Runt was astonished to see that he was only an inch or so taller than his sister. Helen's eyes widened and her hands flew toward her mouth.

"*This* is your brother?"

"Lord, Runt!" Helen finally gasped. "What've you *done* to yourself? Where've you *been?*"

"I . . ." Runt looked down. He didn't want to say in front of Cole.

"Never mind." Helen ran her eyes over him a second time and shook her head. "You'd best put some ice on that eye." She stepped back. "C'mon, now."

Cole rolled his eyes. "We're living in the age of instant communication, and *you* bring home Tom Sawyer!" He retreated into the trailer. "How'd I ever let you talk me into this?"

Runt's neck and ears burned.

"Shower first." Helen pointed to a narrow door. "I'll get you something dry to put on."

Runt hurried forward. The bathroom door weighed almost nothing and shut with a tinny little click. A shimmer of light came through the crosshatched plastic window and allowed him to find the light switch.

Runt took in his surroundings. You'd bump your shoulders turning around in the shower, and the porcelain bowl back home made this toilet look like a toy, but all the necessary equipment was there. He turned to look into the mirror and cringed. The day before yesterday, when Helen had arrived for Ma's funeral, he'd been astonished by their resemblance: the same sandy hair, pointed chin, and lightly freckled skin; the same lanky build, the same hazel eyes.

Now his rain-darkened hair was plastered to his scalp and his swollen left eye was an oily looking purple. Scratches crisscrossed both cheeks and the cut on his chin was caked with blood.

"Runt?" Helen opened the door and laid a set of clothes next to the sink. "Are you all *right?*"

"Yeah."

"That eye must hurt like sixty." She pointed to his chin. "And I don't like the look of that . . ."

"Just needs cleaning," he mumbled.

She gave him a doubtful look and opened the door to the shower. "You pull on this to get water." She twisted a tear-shaped knob. "This way makes it hot and that way makes it cold. Want me to get it started?"

He shook his head.

"Use this for your hair." She handed him a white plastic bottle and pointed to a blue one. "That one's Cole's special stuff."

From his good eye, Runt glowered at the second bottle. Helen didn't have to worry: "Tom Sawyer" wouldn't touch Cole's precious shampoo with a twenty-foot pole.

"Careful, now." Helen tapped the floor of the shower. "It's slippery."

With painful jerks and tugs, Runt peeled his wet clothes away from his bruises. He left them in a heap on the floor and reached for the knob. A gentle yank produced a trickle. He pulled again and freezing water spurted toward him. He twisted the knob and within seconds the water was steaming. He twisted it back, and the water was ice cold again. Why couldn't they have put in *two* faucets? His eyes stung. Why couldn't he be *home*, filling the claw-footed tub and looking forward to a long soak instead of here, in Cole's trailer and this stupid bathroom, being forced to take his first-ever shower?

He emerged from the shower stall feeling a great deal cleaner and a little bit calmer. The cut on his chin had reopened, but with the dried blood gone, it didn't look as bad as it had. He pressed some toilet paper against it, toweled himself, and put on his clothes. He tried to comb his hair with his fingers, but the result was far from satisfactory. He eased open the drawer to the left of the sink and spied a hairbrush. He peered at the bristles: long hairs, the same light brown as his own. It was Helen's, not

Cole's. He brushed his hair, mopped the water from the floor with the towel he had used, and carried his wet laundry into the kitchen.

Helen was filling a pan with water. "You *look* better, anyway." She gave him a small smile. "How're you feeling?"

"All right." He lifted the towel and his clothes. "Where should I put these?"

She pulled a plastic bag from under the sink and held it open. "You can use this for laundry."

He dropped everything into the bag and carried it to the bench that was now his bed. His cardboard box lay on top of it, wide open. Damn! He should have told Helen he'd get his own clothes . . .

"How did you manage," a deep voice demanded, "to get into a fight on your very first day?"

Runt spun around and Cole slowly grinned.

"You don't seem to lack guts." The grin vanished and his eyes grew hard. "But don't go calling attention to yourself."

Runt nodded. If Cole wanted to think he'd gotten banged up in a fight, it was OK with him.

Helen handed Runt a towel filled with ice. "This'll take the swelling down."

Runt gently pressed the towel to his eye.

"How'd it start?" Cole pointed to Runt's bare ankles. "Someone ask you about the flood?"

Runt looked down. The hems of his jeans were a good four inches above the floor.

Cole folded his arms. "Don't you have any clothes that *fit?*"

Runt blushed.

"Now Cole," Helen said quickly. "He just got here . . ."

"Well, he can't go around looking like *that.*" Cole pulled a wallet from his back pocket. "Get him something his size, for God's sake."

Helen looked from the two fifty-dollar bills to her brother. "Tell Cole thank you, Runt!"

Runt clenched his teeth and glued his eyes to the floor. Helen expected him to take *charity* from Cole? And to *thank* him for it?

"Runt!" Helen scolded. "Where're your manners?"

He continued to glower at the floor.

"He's tired." Helen offered Cole an apologetic smile. "I'll take him on Sunday." She held up the money. "This is real nice of you, Cole."

He grunted and checked his watch. "I got business."

Helen followed him to the door. "You have a good night, now."

The truck sputtered to life and she returned to the kitchen. Runt dropped onto his bench and folded his arms.

"Runt?" Helen tipped her head toward the box. "You *need* some new clothes . . ."

"I'll do with what I've got!"

"They're too *small.*" Her voice became soothing. "Kids'll make fun of you at school."

Heat surged up Runt's spine. "I'm not *going* to school!" His good eye widened in surprise. He hadn't planned to say that!

"'Course you are." Helen frowned. "You have to."

Runt scowled. He'd had no choice about Ma dying. He'd had no choice about who would take him. He'd had no choice about this trailer, or the shower, or Cole. But Helen couldn't force him to go to school.

"Don't you want to meet other kids?" she coaxed. "Make some friends?"

"No."

"But, Honeybee . . ."

"Don't call me that!"

Helen's bottom lip trembled. "But I used to, when you were little . . ."

"I'm not *little* anymore!" Runt snapped. "I'm almost thirteen!"

"I know that," Helen protested. "But you've got to go to school till you're sixteen. It's the law." Her eyes grew bright. "And you're *smart,* Runt. You used to do good in school."

Runt's eyes narrowed. He used to do *well* in school. "That was before," he said flatly.

"Before what?"

Runt bit his lip and turned away. Before the babies died. Before you left. Before Mr. McDermott began stopping by once a month to see what other furniture Ma was willing to sell. Before they'd all grown too hungry to think . . .

"I'm not going."

"They'll send a truant officer after you, Runt!"

"No, they won't." He lifted his chin. "How'll they find me? How're they even gonna know I *exist?*"

"They'll find out!" Helen wailed.

Runt shook his head. "They won't. No more'n our old school will come looking. And you can't prove custody."

Helen swallowed hard.

"You try to register me at school and someone'll ask." Runt lifted his chin. Helen was a Remick, wasn't she? And no Remick would stand for charity or outside interference. "You want a bunch of *social workers* crawling all over the place?"

Helen's cheeks turned a shade paler, and Runt knew that he'd won.

4

Helen set two plates on the table, added forks and paper napkins, and turned off the stove. Slouched in his corner, Runt watched her spoon macaroni and cheese onto plates.

"Want ketchup on yours?"

"No."

He'd like the taste of it all right, but he wasn't in a mood to agree to anything Helen suggested. Why had she brought him here anyway? She should have known Cole would just make fun of him.

Helen poured a glass of milk. "C'mon and eat, then."

Runt pushed himself off the bench. The table was the size of a checkerboard, for Pete's sake, and there were only two chairs. Fine—he'd gladly eat somewhere else when Cole was around.

"You want to say grace?"

Runt shook his head. He was thankful for the food in front of him, but he didn't want to hear words from home. Not out loud. Not in this place.

Helen picked up her fork and he did the same. The first warm mouthful slid down into his empty stomach and he paused to relish the sensation. Lord, he was hungry!

"Runt?"

He looked up.

"How come you let Cole think you'd been in a fight?"

Runt frowned. How did Helen know that he hadn't?

"What really happened?"

He shrugged and a sharp pain ripped through his left shoulder. "I fell."

"You *fell?*"

"Down a hill." His eyes narrowed. "But it's none of his business."

"Cole's not a bad person, Runt." Helen hesitated. "He was an only child, and they moved a lot, so he never had much chance to make friends. He's just not used to kids."

Runt squinted at his plate and rapidly moved macaroni from it to his mouth.

"We've *got* to get the clothes." Her voice trembled. "It'll hurt his feelings if we don't."

Runt snorted to himself and speared the last of his macaroni.

"You want some more?"

Runt started to say no, but Helen gave him a hopeful smile and he found himself nodding instead.

She watched him clean his plate a second time and then carried their plates to the sink. "I was *real* worried, Runt . . ."

He squirmed.

". . . when I got home, and Cole told me he hadn't seen you." Her eyes shimmered. "I didn't know if you'd run off, or been hurt . . ."

"How was I supposed to tell you?" Runt folded his arms. "I don't even know where you work!"

Helen pointed to a piece of paper on the square door of the refrigerator. "You didn't see this?"

He shook his head and she handed it to him.

"Dear Runt—I work at Hayden's, at the corner of Washington and Elm . . ." There followed instructions for getting there and a phone number. "There's a pay phone opposite No. 10, and a jar full of change in the cereal cupboard. If you go off exploring, leave me a note, all right?"

"I went out right after you did," he stammered. "I never saw this."

"You didn't *eat?*"

"No."

"And you didn't take anything with you?" Helen shook her head. "Best have that milk, then."

Runt took a large sip and nearly gagged. It was far too thick and sweet.

"It hasn't gone off, has it?" Helen checked the date on the carton. "Should be good till Monday, at least!"

"It hasn't gone off." Runt hesitated. "I just got used to powdered."

"Made thin," Helen said slowly, "with lots of water."

He shrugged very slightly.

"I'm sorry, Runt." She glanced at his cardboard box. "I didn't know things had gotten so bad. Aunt Ruth never told me."

Runt scowled at the table. Until Ma had died, he hadn't known that Aunt Ruth had Helen's address, that *anyone* knew how to reach her. He was suddenly bursting with questions: why did you leave? where did you go? why didn't you ever write?

But asking questions had been frowned upon his whole life, and he couldn't bring himself to ask his sister anything now.

"Nothing you could have done," he mumbled, "even if you *had* known."

Helen sighed and pointed to his glass. "How about half milk and half water, till you get used to regular again?" She gave him a small smile. "You need the calcium. Can't be much longer till you hit your growth spurt."

She poured half the milk back into the carton and topped the glass with water.

"Better?"

He took a sip. "Yeah." He sipped again. "Lots."

"How about we watch some TV?"

Runt glanced at the rain-spattered window. He'd seen enough of the outdoors for today, and what else was there to do? He nodded.

Helen led him through the doorway to the far end of the trailer. The walls were the same brown as the kitchen, but in the light of the floor lamp, they glowed orange. Rain drummed overhead and he looked up. A square window in the ceiling was covered with a bubble of plastic.

"It's called a skylight," Helen said. "It's nice for watching clouds go by."

Runt swallowed past a lump in his throat. The two of them had watched clouds together, a long time ago . . .

"And it makes it feel a little bigger in here."

Runt looked around. A reclining chair was covered in the same striped orange-and-brown fabric as the sofa. To the left were two benches, identical to the ones in the kitchen.

"And here's the TV," Helen said proudly.

Open-mouthed, Runt stared. The screen was more than two feet wide, and the rest of it was only four inches deep! The letters LCD were stamped into its shiny aluminum frame. But where were the knobs for "on/off" and "volume"?

Helen picked up a black rectangle and pushed an orange button. There was a brief, high-pitched whine and the room filled with blue light. A basketball court flared into focus behind an announcer whose sport coat was a vivid green.

"Sharp, ain't it?"

Runt nodded in disbelief. It was sharper than anything he could have imagined. There had been two televisions at school, bulky models set high up on carts. But their colors had been much paler, and their pictures nowhere *close* to this clear . . .

"Here." She handed him the rectangle. "This is the remote. Push on one of these to change channels."

Runt cautiously pressed a button. Nothing happened.

"Sorry," Helen said quickly. "I forgot." She pointed to a glass circle at the top of the remote. "This has to be toward the TV."

Runt aimed and pressed again. The screen winked and a willowy black woman wearing a yellow leotard shimmered into view. He pressed the other button and the basketball announcer reappeared. Runt started to grin but stopped when he felt the cut on his chin pull open.

"Find something you like," Helen urged. "I'll be right back." She picked up an ashtray from the table next to the recliner and carried it to the kitchen.

Runt glanced at the chair. He hadn't seen Helen smoke, so Cole must sit there. He turned toward the sofa. He wasn't going to sit on their bed, even folded up. He eased himself onto the floor and aimed the remote at the TV.

Wink! A floppy-eared beagle raced across a beach. *Wink!* A man with a suitcase argued with a security guard. *Wink!* Wile E. Coyote shot off the edge of a cliff. *Wink!* Runt caught his breath. How could they let people go on TV half-naked like that? And if that was supposed to be dancing . . . *Wink!* His heart leaped: the Tin Man!

"Oh, Runt—it's been ages since I saw that!" Helen's eyes sparkled above her smile. She placed the clean ashtray on the table. "Wanna watch it?"

Runt's eyebrows drew together. Helen liked *The Wizard of Oz?* He looked back to the screen and slowly nodded.

"Let's go all the way, then, and have popcorn! C'mon, and I'll show you how to work the microwave."

He followed her back to the kitchen.

"It's pretty easy." Helen took an envelope from a box and removed the cellophane. "Most everything is labeled with how to cook it." She handed him the package to read.

> This side DOWN.
> Microwave on high 3 to 5 minutes.
> When popping stops, remove from oven IMMEDIATELY.
> HOT!! Open bag carefully, away from face.
> CAUTION: Never leave popcorn unattended in
>   microwave!
> Fire may result.

He gave her a doubtful look. "You sure this stuff is safe?"

She nodded. "Just never put anything *metal* in the microwave. Not even tinfoil, or that shiny paper they put margarine in." She glanced up. "It makes all kinds of sparks."

Runt took a step backward. "I'll just use the stove."

"No, really—it's easy. And fast." She placed the envelope in the microwave and turned the dial to four. A light came on and it began to hum. When the first kernel popped, Helen grinned.

"See?"

Another one popped, and another. Suddenly it sounded as though a string of firecrackers had been set off, and the bag soon doubled in size.

"It's gonna blow up!" Runt hollered. "Turn it off!"

"Wait—it'll be all right. You'll see."

The timer rang. Helen listened closely for a moment, nodded once, and opened the door. The smell of popcorn and salt and something almost like butter filled the tiny kitchen. Holding the bag by one corner, Helen reached for a bowl.

"They're not kidding," she admitted, "about it being hot." She gripped opposite corners, leaned back, and pulled. A cloud of steam rose. When it dispersed, she emptied the bag into the bowl. "See?" She held it toward him. "And no scrubbing burnt oil out of a pan!"

Runt took a piece and cautiously bit down. His eyebrows shot up. "It's good!"

Helen popped a kernel into her mouth. "Not bad," she agreed. "C'mon—we're missing the movie!"

They sat on the floor, eating and watching with rapt attention. When Dorothy and the Cowardly Lion fell asleep among the poppies, Helen said very softly, "This is nice, ain't it?"

Runt was jolted out of Oz and back into Westfield. He was watching a movie with the sister he adored and hadn't seen for nearly half his life. There were a million things to worry about down the road, but this—right now—*was* nice.

"Yeah," he said quietly. "It really is."

5

Runt rolled over, moaned, and lay still again.
Fifteen minutes later, he lifted his head from the pillow and
opened his right eye. It was barely light out, but the trailer was
silent. Had Helen already left for work? He craned his neck.
There was another note on the refrigerator.

Runt wanted to be alone with Cole even less than he had
yesterday. He pushed himself onto one elbow, gasped, and
decided to give his aching limbs five more minutes.

When next he forced open his good eye, bright sunlight was
streaming around the edges of the plastic blinds. He gritted his
teeth and inched himself upright. His swollen hands were almost
frozen in a half-open position and his left eye felt rubbery, like
the white of a hard-boiled egg.

Nearby, a car door slammed and he jumped. Was Cole
still asleep? Runt hauled himself to his feet. Hunching against
the pain, he crept to the middle of the kitchen. The sofa bed
was open, and Cole was in it. Runt glanced at the microwave
clock—1:36!—and then forced himself the rest of the way to the
refrigerator.

"Dear Runt—There's aspirin on the table. Take it easy today.
I'll be home by 4:30. Cole and I are going out tonight, so I'm
bringing something special for your supper. Helen."

BHS SOUTH LIBRARY

Runt read the note a second time and tucked it into his pocket. Sleeping in his clothes hadn't been comfortable, but at least it had saved him from the agony of getting dressed. Wincing, he shoved his feet into his sneakers, tiptoed to the door, and slipped through it.

He pretty much knew what lay to the right, and he couldn't possibly climb down the hill in his present condition. He turned left.

Walking slowly, aching with every step, Runt examined the other trailers. They were identical in size and location of door, and they all had *TrailBilt* in metal script above the front window. But there were differences: an American flag hung above the door of No. 15, and a tricycle was parked near the steps of No. 12. Just as Helen had said, there was a pay phone across from No. 10. Trailers No. 4 and No. 3 appeared to be engaged in a lawn ornament contest between miniature windmills and plastic sunflowers and statues of frogs, and No. 1 had a small patio made of bricks.

He reread the sign at the entrance. Why had they called this place Airview Mobile Home Court? What was "Airview" supposed to mean, anyway? He dismissed the question from his mind and examined the main road into Westfield, a two-lane stretch of gray asphalt with overgrown grass on either side. A semitrailer truck roared by, stirring dust from the road. When it settled, Runt turned to his right and began to walk.

The sun warmed his back and a gentle breeze smelled of clover. As he began to move with greater ease, his spirits rose. So what if Cole didn't like him? He didn't like Cole, either. He'd make it easy on everyone and just stay away from the trailer when Cole was there. And when Cole wasn't around, maybe he and Helen could do things . . .

"Hey, kid!"

A large maroon van was slowing to a stop and the passenger window was sliding down. A moment later, a pale face leaned toward him.

"That shiner's come up *real* good!" Mitch's wide grin appeared. "Too bad I left the digital camera at home!"

Runt looked back to the road.

A gentler voice said, "If your friend is going into town, Mitch, see if he'd like a ride."

The driver of the van was a woman whose face was in shadow but whose hair appeared to be the same carrot color as Mitch's.

"Unlike me, my mother's a kind-hearted soul." Mitch grinned again. "Want a ride?"

"No, thanks."

"Suit yourself, kid!" Mitch said cheerfully. "It *is* nice out. I may even take the Honda for a spin!" Chuckling, he fell back onto his seat as the van rolled forward and picked up speed again.

Runt scowled after it. Was this pest going to pop up wherever he went? He wouldn't show up in a trailer park, that was for sure. His clothes looked expensive, and their van almost new . . .

As Runt resumed walking, his eyes fell upon can after can among the litter by the side of the road. How could people just throw away money like that? He'd passed at least a dollar's worth of cans already. If he'd had anything to carry them in, he'd have picked them up in a minute.

A small black sign with white letters came into view. As he drew closer, the words "WESTFIELD CEMETERY" became visible. An arrow below them pointed to the right. He looked down the winding, tree-lined road and smiled. He couldn't see the cemetery from where he stood, but no matter how far he'd have to walk, he'd never have to slide down that hill again.

He came to a crossroad with a blinking stoplight and turned right. A few minutes later, he passed a road marker announcing his arrival in Westfield. As they'd driven in from Farnham, they'd passed large fields and herds of dairy cows; Runt was surprised to see that Westfield looked more like a small city than it did a farming town. In the distance, he could see office buildings. Close at hand, people hurried along wearing suits and clutching briefcases. He passed a laundromat, a bakery, a secondhand shop, and—best of all—a public library.

Runt checked street signs as he walked: he might as well see where his sister worked. When he came to Elm, he turned left. Two blocks later he spied Hayden's Family Restaurant.

He examined it from across the street. The awning above the front door was faded but securely fastened to its frame. Green gingham curtains covered the lower halves of the windows that looked onto the street; vine-filled planters hung above them. He watched an elderly man with a cane come out, and two men in jeans and plaid shirts go in. It wasn't where rich people would eat, he decided. Tips wouldn't be large, but it looked clean and safe.

How close was it to four o'clock? Runt squinted at the sun and again missed his watch. Helen might have to work for another hour or two . . .

That was it! He'd go to the library. There'd be something to read and somewhere soft to sit. He retraced his steps. The door of the bakery opened, the odor of fresh bread wafted toward him, and his stomach rumbled. He should have squirreled away some food to take with him. Last night, before Cole got home . . .

Runt gritted his teeth. As if Cole's trailer could ever be home!

He climbed up the steps to the library and pulled hard on the door. It rattled but refused to yield. His eyes darted to a card in the window: on Saturdays the library closed at one o'clock. He memorized the hours for the rest of the week and headed back toward the road.

A quarter mile later, his eye caught a glimmer of silver. Groaning a little, he reached down and picked up a dime. Ten cents didn't buy much of anything, but Runt Remick wasn't one to throw money away. He saw another soda can and stopped again. Without something to hold them, he couldn't carry all the cans he'd seen. But he could collect them, and hide them in piles, and come back for them later.

He gathered eight cans before they spilled from his shredded hands back onto the road. He carried them into the long grass, nestled them down, and stepped back. They were completely hidden. How would he find the place? He studied the litter around him. There—a piece of tailpipe. He aligned it with his stash and started off again.

By the time he reached the entrance to the trailer park, he'd collected and hidden forty-three cans. Two dollars and fifteen cents' worth! *Plus* the dime he'd found. It wasn't a fortune, but it was a lot more than he'd had this morning.

Exhausted but satisfied, he sat down near the Airview sign to wait for his sister.

6

"Runt?"

His eyes popped open. Helen was squatting next to him, wearing a concerned frown. "You all right?"

"Yeah."

"What're you doing way down here?"

"Went for a walk." Wincing, he pushed himself to his feet. "Guess it tired me out."

"But why didn't you go back to the trailer?"

Runt's neck grew warm. "Just thought I'd wait for you here." He pointed to the long white bag in her hand. "What's that?"

"A sub."

He wrinkled his nose. A sub-*what?*

"For your supper." She offered him the bag, and the smell of onions made his mouth water.

"Thanks."

"And here's something to go with it!" She grinned and opened her carryall. "Cherry!"

Runt slowly reached for the bottle. Helen *remembered* that cherry was his favorite?

He thrust the sub back into her hands and eagerly twisted the top. Air *whooshed* past plastic to deposit tiny red drops on his hand. The halo of pink foam at the top of the bottle slowly shimmered back down. He closed his eyes and took a long sip. Bubbles danced against the roof of his mouth as the sweet liquid crossed and recrossed his tongue. He finally swallowed—rather loudly.

"Been a while," Helen asked softly, "since you had one of those?"

"Yeah." Runt replaced the cap and gave his sister a smile. "Thanks!"

"I don't make a lot . . ." She handed the sub back to him. ". . . but we'll manage a soda now and then. How's that eye doing?"

"Better," he lied.

"You ice it any today?"

He shook his head.

"Maybe before you go to bed?"

Runt nodded. He might or might not, but he wanted her to stop talking about it.

Helen checked her watch. "I'd best get showered. We've got to leave in an hour."

Runt started to ask where they were going, but the question got stuck in his throat and they walked the rest of the way in silence. When the door banged behind Runt, Cole looked up from the sofa.

"Where've *you* been?"

"Stopped to pick up Runt's supper."

Cole shot a cold glare at Runt. "Almost thirteen, and he don't know how to make a *sandwich?*"

Runt scowled. "I know how."

"Good." Cole swung his legs over the edge of the sofa. "See you learn to *clean up* after yourself!"

"But . . ." Helen's eyebrows drew together.

Cole marched to the kitchen table. "Aspirin don't belong here." He swung his arm toward the bench. "Blanket left all in a heap." He pulled open the door to the bathroom. "And dirt and blood all over in here!"

"I'm sorry, Cole," Helen stammered. "It's my fault. I haven't shown him where the cleaning stuff is."

"He don't need *cleaner* to put things where they belong!"

"I got out the aspirin. He wouldn't have known where to put it." Helen glanced toward the bathroom. "I'll clean up in there after I shower."

Cole shook an index finger at Helen. "Don't you go mopping up after him!" He pointed to the bag in Runt's hand. "You're spoiling him already, and I won't have a brat living here!"

A metallic trilling erupted close at hand. Cole glowered at each of them and went back into the other room. The trilling stopped.

"Yeah?" Cole barked.

Helen raised a finger to her lips.

"Where?" Another brief pause. "Got it." There was a soft snap and Cole reappeared. "Got business." He checked his watch and turned to Helen. "I'll be back in half an hour."

"I'll be sure and be ready."

"And put on something other than that green rag, for God's sake. You look like hell in it."

"All right, Cole. I will."

He banged through the door and Helen's shoulders fell.

"Helen!" Runt sputtered. "He . . ."

"Don't take it the wrong way, Runt. Cole just likes things kept nice." She picked up the aspirin. "You take some this morning?"

Runt shook his head.

"Want any now?"

"No, thanks."

Helen took a spray bottle from under the kitchen sink and the roll of paper towels from its holder. "I'll do up the bathroom after I shower."

"I'll do it." He reached for the paper towels.

Helen shook her head. "But fold the blanket, and put your things in the bench."

Gritting his teeth, Runt did as she asked. He had no problem cleaning up after himself. It was the way Cole had *said* it, the way he'd barked at Helen and seemed to be looking for excuses to find fault with him. And what Cole had said about 'that green rag' was out-and-out *mean* . . .

The bathroom door opened and Helen pointed to the counter. "Ain't you gonna eat?"

Runt looked out the window. He was dizzy with hunger, but he felt sick to his stomach. Helen sighed and moved to the far end of the trailer. There was a sliding sound and the light in the kitchen grew dimmer. Runt got up to look. A door he hadn't noticed the night before had closed off the living room. Its monotonous flatness somehow opened the doors to a loneliness that threatened to consume him. His eyes began to water and he forced himself to take shallow breaths until they were dry again. If he let himself start to cry, he might not be able to stop.

7

He awoke with a throbbing headache. The clock on the microwave read 10:06, and a thick, smoke-scented silence filled the trailer. He'd have heard them come back, wouldn't he?

He tiptoed to the window by the sink and peered out. The truck wasn't there. He flicked the light switch and spied his sandwich. The pain in his head echoed the one in his belly. He needed food. Badly.

The thin loaf of bread was filled with cheese and tomato and onions. He made himself take small bites and chew them slowly. A third of the way through the sandwich, he began to feel more alert. By the time he swallowed the last bite, he felt able to think.

He found a plastic garbage bag and tucked it into one pocket of his jacket. A bag of breakfast cereal went into the other. He turned off the light, retrieved his blanket from the bench, and crawled beneath it. His stomach felt uncomfortably full, but the rest of his body was tingling.

He breathed more and more slowly until a heavy calmness settled over him, a complete absence of doubt: *living here was not going to work.*

It would *never* work. Not with Cole. Not with Helen being pulled in opposite directions between them.

Runt felt a surge of anger at Helen for offering to take him when she should have *known* it wouldn't work. Sighing crossly, he considered his options.

He supposed he could hitchhike back to Farnham. And from there he could go . . . to Aunt Ruth's? Aunt Grace's? They would take him in if he showed up. As family, they would feel they had to. But living with either of them, knowing that he wasn't wanted, wouldn't be a whole lot better than staying here. And Helen didn't ask him to account for himself every minute the way his aunts would . . .

He clenched his fists. It wasn't *his* fault Ma had died. *Or* that his father was dead. Not that his father had ever been much use alive . . .

RUNT WAS SUDDENLY FIVE YEARS OLD AGAIN, ON A STICKY, breezeless August morning. He was sitting on the front steps wondering why Pa had come home for one of his rare overnight visits. The porch door slammed behind Runt and he jumped. The stairs shook as Pa stomped past his older sister Laura and down onto the driveway. By an inch, he missed stepping on Runt.

"Damn!" Pa yelled. "You *stupid,* boy?"

Runt cowered against the bottom step, afraid to speak, afraid to look at Pa's red, unshaven face. Afraid even to breathe.

"Look at you," Pa sneered. "Scrawny, and gutless, with the brains of a lizard." His eyes narrowed and his upper lip curled. "You're the runt of *somebody's* litter, but you're no son of mine!"

Pa lurched down the driveway. Not understanding his father's words, but knowing he'd been dismissed as though dead, Runt crawled under the porch. He stayed there the rest of the day, ter-rified of the bugs and hating the smell of cat urine and rotting wood. Every once in a while Laura called to him through a knot-hole. "Hey, Runt! You still down there?" By the time he emerged at dusk, he had a new name . . .

HE SLOWLY CAME BACK TO THE PRESENT. THAT HAD BEEN THE last time he'd seen his father. For a while, Helen had still called him Robert, and Ma had only ever called him Boy. But Laura had known how much he hated the nickname, and that knowl-edge made her persistent. Mary and Eve had grown up calling him Runt, and finally even Helen had succumbed.

Runt missed Mary and Eve, but he couldn't say he missed Laura. He rolled onto his side and forced his mind back to the question: where could he go? There had to be somewhere . . .

Three hours later, Runt jerked himself awake. Who was laughing?

"Cole!" Helen whispered. "Hush, now."

"He's *asleep,* for God's sake."

Runt quickly closed his eyes.

"Come *on,* woman!"

"Let me just check he's all right."

Footsteps crossed the kitchen. There was a brief pause and then the door to the living room slid closed. Runt heard a loud creak, and then a *thud!* as the sofa bed dropped onto the floor. Cole laughed again and Runt pulled the pillow over his head.

~

HE AWOKE TO THE SMELL OF EGGS COOKING. HELEN WAS AT THE stove, already dressed, her wet hair twisted up onto her head.

"Morning! You sleep?"

He nodded.

"Hungry?"

He nodded again.

"C'mon and eat, then." She put two fried eggs and a slice of bread onto a plate. A glass already stood on the table. Orange juice!

Helen cracked another egg into the pan. "That eye looks better."

Runt discovered that he could open it a bit. He made his way to the table, raised the glass, and inhaled. His stomach fluttered in anticipation. He took a sip and felt his whole body smile.

"Go on, now. While it's hot."

The eggs were perfect: golden brown around the edges, and the middles still runny. Runt savored each bite, wiped the plate with the bread, and savored that, too. He looked up to find his sister smiling at him.

"Keep eating like that and you'll put some meat on those bones!"

Runt scowled at the table.

"That's *good*, Honeyb—" Helen pressed her lips together. "Sorry, I forgot. You're too old for that now."

Runt shrugged very slightly.

"Been doing some thinking," Helen said quickly. "With Cole's hundred, and the thirty I set aside, I figure we can get you two pairs of jeans, three or four shirts and a sweatshirt, and some sneakers." She hesitated. "Your jacket's still all right, ain't it?"

"'S fine."

"Come winter, we'll get you something thicker."

The back of Runt's neck grew warm. Come winter, he wasn't going to *be* here. He didn't know where he'd be, but . . .

"There's a discount store, one of those big chain ones, in Fayetteville," Helen explained. "Takes half an hour to get there, but the prices are really good."

Runt wrinkled his nose. "They open on Sunday?"

Helen nodded. "Eight in the morning to ten at night, every day. Soon as you're washed, we can go."

Helen made several attempts at conversation during their truck ride, but Runt was too filled with resentment about using Cole's money to respond.

They crossed the parking lot, a pair of automatic doors swung open, and Runt followed Helen into brightly lighted chaos. Dozens of shoppers were already pushing red plastic shopping carts along the aisles. A blinking sign invited them to refresh themselves at a snack bar that sold coffee and bagels. The bouncy music overhead was interrupted by a request for customer assistance in Hardware.

Helen turned to Runt. "Little·bigger than Winters', ain't it?"

Runt's good eye darted from sign to sign: Jewelry, Sporting Goods, Housewares, Pharmacy, Toys, Automotive, Electronics . . . What *didn't* this store sell?

"C'mon, then. Let's see what they've got." Helen pulled a shopping cart from a row of twenty and pushed it toward a sign that said Boys.

Runt wrested himself from his daze and hurried after her. They passed a Health Care display and his jaw dropped: they must have thirty kinds of headache remedy for sale! At Winters', there had been only two.

Helen parked the cart next to a shelf filled with denim. "Tens?" She held a pair of jeans to his waist and grinned. "Twelves, but definitely slim!"

Runt blushed.

"How about one pair in blue and one in black?" Helen turned back to the pile. "Black's a little dressier for going anywhere."

Runt stared at the floor. Brand-new pants, and *two* pairs? Who cared what color they were?

"Shirts next." Helen led him to a rack that said Clearance. "Maybe there'll be something your size in here."

Runt stood with his hands in his pockets as she flipped her way around the rack.

"How about these two?" She held up a dark green shirt with a collar and a gray T-shirt with red stripes. "You could keep the green one for special."

Runt swallowed hard. Things must be adding up pretty fast.

Helen added a navy blue polo shirt and a gray sweatshirt to the pile. "Better see where we are . . ."

She paused after reading each tag and squinted in concentration. Finally, she nodded. "We've still got almost forty dollars. Sneakers next?"

Runt chose a pair of black ones and sat down to try them on. The sides felt uncomfortably stiff, but the springy foam inside felt gloriously soft. He stood up and took several steps. He was at least half an inch taller, and he couldn't feel the floor at all!

"Can I have these?"

Helen smiled. "Sure."

Runt put them into the cart and mumbled, "Thanks."

"You're welcome." Helen's manner suddenly became brisk. "Now, we've got *enough,* so don't argue."

Runt looked up in alarm.

"Pajamas . . ." Helen lifted her chin. ". . . and a new toothbrush, and some new underwear."

They found a pair of pajamas on sale for half price, chose a toothbrush, and Helen began peering at the sizes on bags of underwear. Runt frowned. He didn't want new underwear. His old was good enough, and he needed *something* to stay the same. Underwear was private, anyway. No one would see it, so Cole couldn't object . . . Helen tossed a bag into the cart and Runt set his jaw. He just wouldn't wear them. She'd never know.

Helen added up their purchases a second time and calculated the tax. "A hundred twenty-seven eighty," she announced with a grin. "We made it!"

Runt gave her a weak smile in return. "You're good at figuring."

She blushed. "Got to be, waiting tables."

At the checkout they waited in line behind an elderly man with eight flowerpots and a tall woman with three videotapes and a roll of wrapping paper. Her credit card had expired, and she rummaged through her purse for another one.

Runt let his eyes wander. They fell upon a plastic digital watch. The price tag read $2.49, and Runt's heart leaped. That was sixty cents less than the underwear!

"Found it!" The woman held up her new card in triumph and the cashier swiped it through her machine.

Helen turned to Runt. "Put things on so the stripes are up." She placed a shirt on the conveyer belt and turned the tag so the UPC code faced the ceiling. "Like this."

Runt took a quick breath. "Please?" He pointed to the watch. "Can we put the underwear back and get this instead?"

Helen looked from Runt to the watch and back again. "But you need new . . ."

Runt shook his head hard. "No I don't. *Please?*"

She pursed her lips but pulled the watch from the display. "If it's all that important to you . . ."

"Thanks!"

The clerk flashed her little red light over the tags, and in less time that it would have taken one of the Winters to ring up a single purchase, Runt's clothes had been bagged and Helen was collecting her change.

Runt spent the ride back to Westfield reading the instructions and setting his new watch. As they pulled up to the trailer, he fastened it onto his wrist with a satisfied grin.

"Put on something new, all right?" Helen gave him an encouraging smile. "Cole'll want to see what we got."

Runt's grin became a scowl. He'd put on the new clothes to keep peace. But the money for his sneakers and his watch had come from Helen, and he'd be wearing his *own* underwear.

8

Runt emerged from the bathroom feeling unsteady.
The waistband of his new jeans had slipped past his hips—he'd
have to find something to use as a belt—and the seams of the
gray T-shirt were scratchy. And although the insides of his new
sneakers were blissfully soft, their stiff soles forced him to shuffle.
Having gotten used to feeling the terrain underfoot, he found it
unsettling not to be able to.

"Don't you look nice!" Helen beamed at him from the sofa.

"Damned sight *better,* anyway." Cole stubbed out a cigarette
and blew a long stream of smoke into the air. "Human, at least."

Runt felt the muscles in his shoulders tighten.

"You've got your sister's features, and she's not bad looking . . ."

Runt blinked. Was that supposed to be a compliment?

". . . when she takes the time to fix herself up. See you don't
go tearing holes in those things."

"He'll take care of them." Helen gave Runt a reassuring smile.
"It's almost time for the game, Cole. You put it on, and I'll fix us
some lunch."

Cole lifted his chin toward the TV. "You watch baseball?"

Runt shook his head. Back home, there hadn't been anything
on which to watch baseball—or anything else. The television had
gone three years ago.

"You should." Cole picked up the remote. "It's a thinking man's game." He rapidly changed channels. "Winners take intelligent risks," he said smugly. "Losers take stupid ones."

Cole seemed to be talking about more than baseball, but Runt had no idea what. Helen came back into the room and handed Cole a bottle of beer.

He grunted and gave her a nod of approval. Helen smiled at him and returned to the kitchen. Cole twisted the top from the bottle and took a sip. "Have a seat. Learn something."

Runt hiked up his pants and sat down on the floor. Was it possible that Cole was trying to be nice?

The national anthem began and Runt resisted the impulse to get to his feet—it was plain that Cole wasn't going to. A blonde woman in a purple pantsuit threw out the first pitch. Although the ball barely made it over the plate, the crowd cheered wildly.

"Waste of time," Cole muttered.

"Play ball!"

Runt watched the game, not out of interest, but because it would have been too awkward to leave. When it finally ended, Cole turned to Helen. "I'll give you this much about your brother. He doesn't ruin a game by babbling through the whole thing."

Runt's cheeks grew warm. His silence certainly hadn't been out of respect. Not for a game that was 4 percent action and 96 percent boredom!

Once again Cole announced that he "had business" and left the trailer. Runt decided to take a nap. At suppertime, he got up long enough to eat a bowl of spaghetti and went right back to sleep.

He awakened before dawn feeling better than he'd felt in a long time. The swelling in his left eye had gone down, and the aching in his body had lessened considerably. He felt oddly alert, a combination of having eaten three solid meals in a single day and having slept the better part of sixteen hours overnight. It had been an awfully long time since he'd done either one of those things, and even longer since he'd done both.

He dressed silently, tying his jeans around his waist with a piece of clothesline Helen had found. He tucked his blanket into the bench and quickly scribbled a note telling Helen he'd gone exploring and would be back by five. He fixed it to the refrigerator with a magnet and slipped through the door. Walking briskly, he headed for the road.

He collected the cans he'd hidden on Saturday and checked his watch: 6:40. The cemetery gate wouldn't open for another hour and twenty minutes. A semitrailer roared past him in the opposite direction, and his eyebrows shot up. No reason people should throw cans on only one side of the road . . .

At 7:54 he hid a bag containing five dollars and thirty-five cents' worth of cans in a patch of tall grass and began his walk down the tree-lined road. The dawn's orange light had long since become a pale yellow, but the air remained fresh and cool. Runt looked with appreciation at springtime's changes: where branches had been bare, there were now buds; where there had been buds, there were now lime green leaves; where there had been only leaves, there were now pastel blossoms.

The gate was open. Beyond it, Runt spied a stooped, gray-haired man pushing a rusty wheelbarrow. He remained where he was until the man disappeared behind the stone building.

He followed the same route he'd taken on Friday. When he spied the drinking fountain, he looked around cautiously. He felt good, but not so good that he wanted an orange-haired ghoul sneaking up on him . . .

Mitch did not appear, and Runt decided he would explore the older part of the cemetery first, the part with the big trees. When he reached the bench near the far fence, he took off his sneakers and socks. There were blisters on both his heels. He drained them, pressed the skin down, and then lost himself in the quiet.

When his stomach growled, he pulled the cereal from his pocket and quickly ate it. Then, new shoes in hand, he strolled toward a collection of pale gray markers that listed beneath the arms of a craggy maple.

These were truly ancient headstones, many of them too weathered to read what had been carved upon them. Several of them were cracked, and all of them were covered with something that looked like gray moss but which crumbled to dust at his touch. Runt paused in front of one that read:

BRECKNER

DIED

Whoever this person had been, whatever he or she might have done or accomplished, one thing was certain: Breckner had, indeed, died.

For no reason he could have explained, Runt decided that Breckner had been female. Had she withered away, like his mother? Had she died of exposure, like his father? Had she been lost as a baby, like Mercy and Hope?

Or had Breckner grown up to become a mother herself? Were her descendants living nearby? Would they know, or care, who she had been? Whether she'd been kind or cruel? Whether she'd invented something, or swindled someone, or championed some noble cause? He shook his head. Most likely, no one knew. Most likely, it mattered not one bit that Breckner had ever been alive.

He passed a dozen similarly weathered headstones before stopping again.

At Rest
Louisa Houck
died Jul. 19, 1874
AET 4 days

Runt squinted at the stone. Four days? What reason could there have been for little Louisa Houck to even have been born? Except to give heartbreak to her parents, and cost them the price of a burial . . .

Runt sighed. Mercy had died at nineteen months. She had wandered off and been found in a neighbor's pond. Ma hadn't let them see her body, and Runt's memory of Mercy was of a sweet, laughing toddler: there one morning at breakfast, gone forever before lunch.

And Hope had at least lived four months—long enough to learn how to smile and play peekaboo. Runt's eyes filled with tears. He *wanted* to remember Hope's toothless grin, the way she had gurgled happily when he called her name. But those memories were trapped behind the moment when he'd reached down to touch her cheek and found it cold.

"Crib death," Ma had called it, citing "the Lord's will." The doctor who wrote the death certificate had called it something else, some kind of "syndrome," but whatever he'd called it, it hadn't mattered. Hope was gone, too . . .

And there had been no good-byes. Not to the babies, not to Helen. Ma had refused to let them attend Mercy's funeral, and later refused to let them attend Hope's. Six days after Hope died, Ma had announced that Helen was "no longer welcome in this house," and they were not to speak her name again.

Runt wondered if he'd ever find out what had happened between Helen and Ma. Even more than that, he wanted to know why Helen had never written. Despite the six years between them, they'd been terribly close . . .

"Hey, kid!"

Runt leaped sideways and swore. Not *him* again!

"You've got a real thing for cemeteries, don't you?" Mitch grinned. "I'll have to let the truant officer know where to find you!"

"He finds me," Runt retorted, "he finds you!"

Mitch shook his head. "I'm legally absent. I'm on a medical."

Runt scowled. A medical what?

"Don't get yourself in a knot, kid. I don't rat on people." Mitch grinned again. "Besides, Westfield doesn't *have* a truant officer!"

Runt continued to scowl, but some of the fear in his stomach dissolved.

"Seriously, kid." Mitch pushed a button and the wheelchair rolled forward. "Where you from?"

"Nowhere!"

"Some place damned unfriendly, that's for sure."

Pinpricks crawled up the back of Runt's neck.

"What are you afraid of, kid? A few minutes' conversation?" Mitch brought the chair to a halt. "Or that I'm going to jump you and swipe your wallet?"

"Mornin', Sport!"

Minus his wheelbarrow, but carrying a small spade, the gray-haired man was coming toward them. His arms and legs moved in a series of awkward jerks, but he walked at a surprisingly brisk pace.

"Hey, Noah!"

"You're out early today." The man stopped in front of the wheelchair. He didn't smile, but Runt thought he might have winked. Noah's white eyebrows were in constant motion and his face was so full of wrinkles that it was difficult to tell. "Who's this?" He jerked his head toward Runt.

"This?" Mitch's eyes widened in mock surprise, and Runt caught a glimpse of pale blue above his dark circles. "This is my new best friend!"

Noah frowned. "He got a name?"

Runt fixed his narrowed eyes on Mitch. Go ahead, wise guy. Tell him.

Mitch grinned. "Isadore!"

"Hmmph!" Noah glared at Runt. "Sounds like a girl's name."

"That's not my name!"

Mitch roared with laughter and Noah shook his head.

"Dunno why I bother asking you anything, Sport. Knowed you two years, and nary a straight answer yet."

Mitch wiggled his hairless eyebrows. "Never give up hope!"

"Not likely, you little devil." One corner of Noah's mouth twitched. "You done too much teaching on that."

A bit of color crept into Mitch's pale, puffy cheeks and he cleared his throat. "Who you digging up today, Noah?"

Runt's stomach flip-flopped. This old man wasn't really going to *unbury* someone, was he?

"Haven't had a gander at Maybelle Wills in a while . . ."

This time Runt saw the wink.

". . . but she'll have to keep. Mrs. Trenbleth's decided to do some planting around the Major's stone."

Mitch nodded. "Say hi to them both for me."

"Will do." He squinted at Runt and aimed a forefinger at Mitch. "Keep your eyes open around this guy, Isadore. Never say I didn't warn you about him."

Mitch burst out laughing. "Warned him myself, Noah!"

Runt blinked. Mitch *had* warned him.

"Hmmph!" Noah made a wry face. "From the guy who sells ice cubes to Eskimos." He shouldered his spade. "Got to get on. Some of us have to work for a living."

"Bye, Noah."

Runt watched Noah's jerking gait until he disappeared.

"So, kid," Mitch demanded. "If it isn't Isadore, what is it?"

9

He almost said Runt. It was there, on the tip of his tongue. But for some reason he mumbled, "Robert."

"Robert, huh?" Mitch sat back and tipped his head. "Maybe . . ."

Runt's eyes narrowed again. Maybe *what?!* He ought to know his own name, for Pete's sake!

Mitch nodded. "There might be some Robert the Bruce in you . . ."

"Who's he?" Runt blurted out, and immediately wished that he hadn't.

Mitch sat up taller. "One of the most famous kings of all time. He freed Scotland from control by the English."

Runt snorted in disgust. He was about as much Robert the Bruce as his tormentor was an Olympic athlete. He looked at Mitch again. Maybe he was getting used to his appearance. He didn't look as scary as he'd looked the other day.

"How'd you learn about Robert the Bruce?"

"Did a project on him in fifth grade."

Runt suddenly wondered how old Mitch was. "What grade you in now?"

"I should be in eighth, but I've missed a lot of school. Technically, I'm in seventh." He leaned forward with a determined look. "But I'm going to try to finish eighth grade over the summer."

"How come?"

Mitch looked down at his hands. "So I can start high school with my friends in the fall."

"Oh." Runt's eyebrows drew together. If Mitch wasn't in school, and if he wasn't with his friends, then he must be pretty lonely. Runt knew how that felt. He'd been that lonely after Helen had left . . .

"What do you do when you're not in school?"

Mitch rolled his eyes. "You mean apart from doctors' appointments and clinics, and visits from nutritionists and psychologists, and all the rest of it?"

The bitterness in Mitch's voice was startling, and he suddenly looked scary again.

"Um . . . yeah." Runt swallowed hard. "Apart from that."

Mitch gave him a wicked grin. "I cause trouble!"

The return of Mitch's usual demeanor was reassuring, and Runt smiled back. "You cause trouble?"

Mitch nodded. "Stir things up. Keep 'em from getting too dull."

"How?"

Mitch shook his head. "I'm not giving away all my secrets. Not *that* easy." He grinned again. "Not even to my new best friend!"

Runt bit his lip. What was he supposed to say to that?

Beep! Beep! The maroon van that had passed Runt on the road to Westfield was wending its way toward them.

"I've got ward duty this afternoon." Mitch reached for the control box on his wheelchair. "But some other time, maybe you could come over."

He rolled toward the narrow platform that was descending from the van. Runt watched with admiration as Mitch maneuvered his chair into place and backed it onto the lift.

"Hello!"

A woman came around the front of the van and smiled. Runt's first impression was of a plump, cuddly teddy bear wearing a Penn State sweatshirt. Her hair was the same bright orange as Mitch's, but it was much thicker and streaked with gray. She was pretty, Runt decided, even though she looked as though she could use some sleep.

"I'm Maureen Curran. Mitch's mom." She put out her hand.

Clumsily, Runt took it. "Rr . . . Robert." He swallowed. "Robert Remick."

She smiled again. "Pleased to meet you, Robert!"

"Hey!" Mitch called. "No fair! She got *two* names out of you on the first try." He grinned. "You're gonna give me a complex or something!"

Mrs. Curran rolled her eyes. "I wouldn't go throwing stones, Mitch. Not with *your* record for driving people insane!"

Mitch put a melodramatic wrist to his forehead. "Maligned at every turn," he sighed. "By even my nearest and dearest . . ."

His mother kissed his cheek and locked the wheelchair into place. *"Someone's* got to keep you in line!" She pushed a button inside the van and the chair began to rise.

Mitch grinned and raised one hand in the peace sign. "See ya, Robert!"

Mrs. Curran secured the van door, smiled again at Runt, and climbed behind the wheel. The ignition caught and in moments they were gone.

Runt stared after the van. What, exactly, was wrong with Mitch? And what on earth was "ward duty?" How had he even gotten into another conversation with him? He certainly hadn't intended to . . .

Even though Mitch would be elsewhere for the afternoon, Runt had had enough of the cemetery. He'd redeem his roadside findings and get something to eat, and then maybe he'd see what the library was like.

A teenager wearing headphones and bobbing in time to his music counted Runt's cans, swept them into a plastic bag, and laid five dollars and thirty-five cents on the counter. Runt pocketed the money and turned his attention to what he might buy. The ready-made sandwiches looked delicious, but none of them cost less than three dollars, and even a bottle of water cost sixty-nine cents. Runt settled on a single large cookie that cost a quarter. He hoped the library would have a drinking fountain.

In front of the library stood a large maple tree. Runt nestled himself among its roots, slowly peeled the wrapper from the cookie, and took a large bite. Three bites later it had vanished, and he hurried up the steps. The door yielded easily this time, and he stepped from bright sunlight into soothing dimness. High ceilings, white walls, and dark blue carpet everywhere. Half a dozen upholstered chairs in front of three magazine racks. Oak shelves lined with thousands of books, each one inviting him to open it.

This library was much nicer than the one at his old school, but it was similar enough to be comforting. As money had grown more and more tight, as there had been fewer options and extras, books had become Runt's refuge. As long as you returned things when they were due, it didn't cost anything to be transported to other places and times, to read about people whose troubles were greater than your own. And, unlike real life, *book* people almost always triumphed in the end.

Feeling suddenly homesick for old friends, for *Treasure Island* and *Captains Courageous* and *The Lost Prince,* Runt's eyes darted around the room in search of a card catalog. He found none. There were six computers around a hexagonal table. A sign above it read "Electronic Book Search." Beneath it was a smiling face and the announcement: "Our catalog is now on computer!"

Runt's shoulders fell. He didn't know how to use a computer. What was wrong with cards in drawers, for Pete's sake?

"I'm sorry, young man." A middle-aged woman offered him an apologetic smile. "Our computers are down today. May I help you find something?"

"No, thanks."

Runt ducked past her and hurried toward the Young Adult section. He eventually found *Treasure Island* and spent a happy afternoon reading before his watch alarm rang. Was it already four fifteen? He checked the clock behind the librarian's desk. It was.

Wishing he could take it with him, Runt reluctantly reshelved the book. He couldn't apply for a library card. For starters, he didn't even know the zip code of Cole's trailer. And he didn't have anything to prove that he lived there. As far as the world at large was concerned, he didn't live anywhere . . .

Runt sighed. He'd told Helen he'd be back by five. He'd better get moving.

10

Runt stopped outside the trailer. The truck wasn't in its usual place. Please, *please* let Helen be home. *Please* let it be Cole who's gone off.

He knocked lightly and opened the door.

"That you, Runt?"

"Yeah."

"I'm glad." His sister looked up from the sink and smiled. "What you been doing all day?"

Runt hesitated. Helen's question contained none of Cole's condescension, none of Aunt Grace's suspicion, none of Aunt Ruth's concern for what the neighbors might think. She sounded genuinely *interested,* and he felt suddenly shy.

"Exploring." He pointed to the note he'd left on the refrigerator.

"Thanks for leaving that." She turned back to the sink. "But there's nothing much to explore around here. It's not like back home."

Runt wrinkled his nose. Helen remembered their rambling walks through the woods? She still thought of Farnham as home?

"Cole's gone out, so it's just you and me for supper." She lifted a colander from the sink. "How about franks-and-beans and a salad?"

"Sounds good."

"Wash up, and you can do the carrots, all right?"

Runt rinsed his face and examined it in the mirror. The scratches had faded to pale pink and the cut on his chin was now a thin line. His left eye was still pretty swollen, but the purple had become a yellowish green. Another week or so, and he'd look like himself again. He scrubbed his hands with soap, wiped the sink clean, and returned to the kitchen.

He cut two carrots before giving in to temptation. He popped a thin orange circle into his mouth and paused to enjoy it.

"I'm glad it's just you and me tonight." Helen emptied a can of baked beans into a pan. "Gives us a chance to talk."

Runt resumed slicing. "'Bout what?"

"You eating, for one thing." She turned on a burner and took a package of hot dogs from the refrigerator. "How come you didn't have anything for breakfast?"

Runt frowned. How did she know that he hadn't? He shrugged. "Didn't want to wake Cole."

"You're not going to wake anybody pouring milk on cereal. You've *got* to eat right," she pleaded. "You're growing, and you'll get sick if you don't." Helen looked back to the stove. "There's money for food, but nothing left over for doctors."

Runt pushed down hard on the knife and the carrot flew from the counter to the floor. Helen retrieved it, rinsed it, and held it toward him.

"Promise you'll eat?"

Without looking at her, he accepted the carrot and nodded.

"Good." She stirred the beans. "You take off before sun up so I couldn't argue about school?"

Runt shifted restlessly. "We already talked about that."

"You need an *education*, Runt. You want to end up like me? Hoping for fifty-cent tips?"

"I'll find some other kind of job."

"Without even graduating eighth grade?" Helen's voice rose. "Doing *what*, Runt? You can't even get working papers till you're fourteen!"

Runt's knuckles grew white above the knife's handle. "I'm not going."

Helen threw up her hands. "What're you going to *do* all day?"

"I'll find something," Runt growled. "And I *won't* cause you trouble."

"That ain't what's worrying me!" Helen shook her head. "Maybe I shouldn't have brought you here . . ."

Runt's chin quivered. "Why *did* you?"

Helen did not reply and he finally looked up. Her eyes were brimming with tears.

"Because I know what it's like . . ." She swallowed hard. ". . . to feel you're not welcomed by family." She turned away. "And I didn't want that for you."

Runt's throat began to ache.

"I *care* about you, Runt. If I'd thought you'd be better off with Aunt Ruth or Aunt Grace, I wouldn't have offered."

"If you care so much, how come you never wrote?" Runt's chest heaved. "Not ever. Not even *once!*"

"But I *did* write!" Helen wailed. "I wrote *lots,* and you never answered!"

Runt's eyes began to burn.

"Ma never gave you my letters?" Helen's voice wavered.

Runt shook his head. "And I couldn't write *you*. I didn't know where you'd gone. None of us knew Aunt Ruth had your address until after Ma died."

Tears spilled down Helen's cheeks. "I'm sorry," she whispered. "I should've known Ma wouldn't give you anything from me. I should've sent things to school, or to Winters'."

Their eyes met.

"Why?" Runt croaked.

"Why'd Ma kick me out?"

He nodded.

Helen began to tear lettuce. "I was crying about Hope, and Ma told me to stop. Crying wouldn't change things, she said, and Hope dying was the Lord's will."

Runt winced.

"And I said it'd been bad enough losing Mercy . . ." Helen's voice became hoarse. ". . . but if it was the Lord's will to strike a sleeping baby, then I didn't *believe* in the Lord anymore."

THE ROOM LURCHED. RUNT WAS SIX, STANDING IN THE KITCHEN back home, unable to believe the flat, dark words coming from his mother's mouth. "She is no longer welcome in this house."

THE SOUND OF HELEN SOBBING PULLED RUNT BACK TO THE present. He wanted so much to help her, to say something that would make her feel better, but he had no idea what that might be. Dark yellow smoke began to rise from the pan. Runt took it from the burner and turned off the stove.

"Helen?"

Her shoulders heaved sharply and her crying grew softer. "Ma was wrong."

She sniffed loudly and looked up.

"She pushed you out and left you to fend for yourself when you were already hurting as bad as could be."

A wave of fresh tears erupted and Helen nodded. "That's just how it was, Runt." She pulled a paper towel from the roll and wiped her eyes. "Thanks for understanding that."

"Not having you home hurt *us* bad, too," he mumbled. "I missed you something fierce."

Helen sniffed again. "Laura didn't help much, did she?"

No, Laura hadn't been any help. Laura had been *worse* than no help. She'd called him a baby and told him to stop moping, and then spent every moment she could away from home—leaving him to look after Mary and Eve. Runt squared his shoulders and shook his head.

Helen sighed and poked at the beans. "Charred up supper pretty good, didn't I?"

Runt mustered a small smile. "It'll taste like a cookout."

Helen laughed. "You got a long memory, Runt. Only cookout I remember back home was that time Ma took us to visit her friend. To that big white house by the lake. Remember?"

Runt squinted into the distance and nodded.

Helen opened the refrigerator. "What kind of salad dressing you want?" Glass clinked against glass. "We got Thousand Island and Creamy Italian."

"You pick."

"Then let's have Thousand Island. It's already open."

They filled their plates and carried them to the table.

"Ugh." Helen swallowed a mouthful of beans and reached for her iced tea. "That's *pitiful!*"

"No, it ain't," Runt argued. "Put some ketchup on it."

Helen shook her head. "You must be near to starved if you can eat that."

Runt continued to eat. He *was* hungry, and even without ketchup, the franks and the beans tasted good.

"You're sweet not to mind." Helen gave him a small smile. "Cole'd have a conniption if I ever served him something burnt."

Runt savagely forked salad into his mouth. He hated the way Cole talked to Helen. He was critical, and demanding, and out-and-out *spoiled*.

"How come you moved in with him, anyway?" Runt froze. He hadn't meant for that to come out!

"Seemed the best thing at the time." Helen shrugged. "Aunt Ruth wrote me that Ma wouldn't make it through spring, and they wouldn't have let us share a room at the boardinghouse."

Runt's chest grew tight. "Us" didn't mean Helen and Cole— that had nothing to do with Ma dying. By "us," Helen meant the two Remicks . . .

A wave of nausea swept from Runt's knees to his neck. It was on account of *him* that Helen was with Cole. She'd moved into the trailer so she could offer a home to her brother!

11

Runt flopped from his side onto his stomach,
wadded his pillow into a ball, and slammed his cheek down. His
sister was with a man (Ma would have called it "living in sin")
who didn't even *treat* her right, and she was doing it to put a roof
over her brother's head.

Runt's chest heaved in frustration. It wasn't as though he'd
had any say in the matter. He hadn't even *known* about it. But it
still felt like Helen's being with Cole was his fault.

He'd never given up hope completely, but little by little,
he'd built a wall against not hearing from Helen, a wall that
kept his loneliness from eating him alive. Finding out that she
had written was forcing him to remember how much her leaving had hurt.

And that pain was magnified by the new knowledge that
Ma had kept Helen's letters from him. Six years of believing
that she didn't care. Six years of believing he wasn't *worth* caring
about . . .

And now that he knew the truth? He sighed wearily. Ma was
dead and all of that was in the past. He needed to focus on what
to do next.

He'd already decided to leave, hadn't he? He just hadn't figured out where to go. If he wasn't here, Helen wouldn't be stuck trying to defend him. If he wasn't here, she wouldn't have any reason to keep living with Cole . . .

A breeze came through the window and rattled the blinds. Runt glared at them. Being homeless would be better than living in this plastic box! He rolled over and sighed again. Not when it was raining, it wouldn't.

He fell into a restless sleep and dreamed that he was searching for Helen in the woods back home. He could hear her calling him, but no matter how hard he tried, he couldn't see her.

He awoke the next morning full of resolve. Wherever he ended up deciding to go, he'd need money to get there. Even if he hitchhiked back to Farnham, he'd have to eat along the way. Besides, it would be only fair to offer anyone who picked him up some money for gas.

Without working papers, he couldn't even get a part-time job. He'd have to offer his services on a per-job basis. He could ask store owners if they'd be willing to pay him to sweep sidewalks or stack boxes. He'd have to stick to weekends for now, but when school let out for the summer, he could work every day. In the meantime, he'd collect cans and redeem them. It wouldn't make him a fortune, but it would be something to do. If he could find twenty cans every day, he'd be another dollar ahead each night.

The first day of his new plan was a profitable one. He collected sixty-two cans along the road to the left of the Airview sign. He returned home exhausted, but three dollars and ten cents richer. The following day, he walked a mile and a half along the same road before he found his first can. His take for that day was a mere seventy cents. On Thursday he tried the road leading to Westfield from the south and pocketed almost five dollars. Friday morning he decided to take a vacation from collecting cans, in the hope that by Monday there would again be enough of them to make all that walking worthwhile.

When Helen left for work, he ate a bowl of cereal, washed and dried the dish, and made himself a sandwich. He'd kept his promise about eating, and he was feeling physically and mentally stronger than he'd felt for a long time. He'd explore some more of the cemetery, he decided. And if Mitch showed up? Runt shrugged. It wouldn't kill him to listen for a few minutes . . .

In fact, it would be kind of nice to hear someone talk. After their exchange about Ma and the letters, Helen and he had retreated into embarrassed silences. Remicks didn't ask questions. Remicks didn't talk about things much at all, and never, *ever* about how they were feeling. Runt knew he was wrestling with what he'd learned, with the fact that six years had been a lie, and he wondered whether Helen was struggling with the same thing.

At the cemetery gate he focused his attention on the physical surroundings. The changes that had taken place in three days were astounding. There were now leaves on almost all the trees, and a few had already darkened to deep green. Many of the flowering trees had shed their blossoms, and puffs from cottonwood trees swooped and swirled in the breeze. It was definitely still spring, but there were signs that summer wasn't far away.

Runt spied Noah's wheelbarrow up ahead and took a path in the opposite direction. He walked for fifteen minutes before he began meandering among the headstones. The markers were much larger here than they were near the far fence, and they ranged in color from a gray that sparkled in sunlight to a deep pink lined with white veins. He paused before one on which two wedding rings were entwined.

DEWITT

FATHER LAVERNE 1925–1991

MOTHER HADINA 1929–

Poor old Hadina, whoever she was, was probably in a nursing home by now. Runt wondered whether she missed Laverne, or whether—despite the carved wedding rings—she'd been relieved when he died.

Runt had certainly felt relieved when he'd learned that his father was dead. Ma hadn't said anything, of course, except that it was the Lord's will. But Runt hadn't thought his mother had seemed at all sad. It was pitiful, he decided now, to have had a man's children and not to feel sorry he'd died . . .

"Hi! Boy!" Noah was hurrying toward him with his strange jerking gait. "Got a message for you."

Runt wrinkled his nose. A message? From whom? About what? Noah must have him mixed up with somebody else.

The old man came to a halt an arm's length away. When his wheezing subsided, he pulled a piece of paper from his shirt pocket. "From Sport!"

Runt hesitated. This Mitch kid sure was persistent . . .

"He's had a couple of bad days." Noah cast his eyes down. "You know what I mean."

Runt had no idea what Noah meant, but rather than say so, he accepted the paper.

"His mom dropped it off *Wednesday,*" Noah scolded. "Been keeping an eye out for you ever since!"

Runt scowled. What right did this old man have to holler at him? He hadn't said he'd be back any particular day, or any special time . . .

"You tell him that," Noah's voice became husky. "You tell Sport from me, he's a royal pain in the behind!" He stomped back in the direction from which he had come and Runt unfolded the paper.

"To Robert the Bruce," he read. "The treacherous English have me surrounded, and I could stand some rescuing by a rogue king. (My allies remain loyal but are imprisoned by the Villains of Academe.)"

Below that was a map, and farther down, Mitch had scribbled his name. At the bottom of the page, in an even script, a few lines had been added: "Dear Robert—You don't have to stay a long time, but please come if you can. Anytime between ten and two. Mrs. Curran."

Runt looked up from the paper and let his eyes wander. Maybe cutting school *was* making him stupid. He understood Mitch's note even less than he'd understood Noah!

He checked his watch. It was 9:43. He reread the note and, wondering why he felt compelled to do so, began to follow the map.

It was carefully drawn and clearly labeled, and in less than half an hour he stood in front of 563 Peppertree Drive. The maroon van was parked in the driveway, and a long cement ramp led to the front porch, so this had to be the right place.

The house was made of dark red brick and its diamond-paned windows opened outward instead of sliding up. Some kind of ivy had climbed to the top of the chimney. The lawn was wide and weedless. The bushes below the porch were neatly trimmed, and drifts of white and purple impatiens lay in front of them.

He checked his watch again. It was 10:12, and there was no reason not to knock. He walked up the path feeling glad that he wasn't wearing his old clothes. He raised the brass knocker but then carefully lowered it back into place. It weighed a ton and would make a whole lot more noise than he cared to make. He gave the door a couple of raps with his knuckles.

"Just a minute!" A moment later, the door opened and Mrs. Curran's face lit up. "Robert! Come in, come in!" She waved him forward. "Mitch will be so glad to see you."

"Uh, hi, Mrs. Curran." Runt stepped past her and she closed the door. "I would have come yesterday," he stammered, "but I didn't get the note until this morning."

"We'll make it easier from now on, and arrange things by phone. Be sure to give Mitch your number before you go, OK?"

Mrs. Curran crossed a floor of polished wood and began climbing a curving set of stairs. The carpet that covered the steps was pale gray, and Runt stared at it in horror. He'd been tramping around in wet grass, and the treads on his new sneakers just *collected* mud . . .

He quickly pried off his shoes, placed them next to the wall, and hurried after Mitch's mother. She reached the second floor landing and turned to her right.

"Mitch?" she called. "I've got a surprise for you!"

12

"Oh, NO!" Mitch wailed. "Not Cobra Colandra!"

Mrs. Curran stepped through the doorway and put her hands on her hips. "It *isn't* Doctor Colandra, and you are *not* to call her The Cobra!"

Runt suppressed a smile. Mrs. Curran wasn't scolding as if she meant it, and he was certain Mitch would go right on calling his doctor a snake.

"Then what's my surprise?"

Mrs. Curran turned to Runt. "He doesn't *deserve* company, but come and say hi anyway!"

Runt took three tentative steps forward. Mitch was lying in a bed with metal railings. He was propped against two large pillows, his tufts of hair a ridiculous orange halo above his head. The circles beneath his eyes looked almost black.

"Halt!"

Runt froze. There was no trace of a smile on Mitch's face.

"You frisk him for syringes?"

Mrs. Curran rolled her eyes. "Robert's come all this way to see you, and you can't even say hello before you start cracking jokes?" She picked up a squirt gun and offered it to Runt. "You're welcome to use Mitch for target practice!"

Runt risked a glance at the bed. Mitch's grin wasn't as wide as it usually was, but it still nearly split his face in two.

"Come on." Mrs. Curran returned the squirt gun to the top of the dresser. "Let's get you cranked up, and then maybe you can *pretend* to be civilized." She pressed a button somewhere and the head of the bed began to rise.

Mitch winked at Runt. "I'll try to fake it."

The bed stopped moving and Mrs. Curran pulled a chair away from a computer table. "If you're going to put up with this guy, Robert, the least we can do is offer you a seat." She paused in the doorway. "I'll be up in a little while."

"So!" Mitch waved a hand toward the chair. "Take a load off. Tell me what's new."

Runt edged his way between the desk and the wheelchair and sat down. A plastic bag half filled with yellow liquid hung from one of the bed rails, and a narrow tube ran from it under the blanket. Runt's cheeks grew warm. Was that how the poor kid had to pee? He forced his eyes away from the bag.

"Nothing much."

"Ehhhnt!" Mitch made a shrill buzzing sound. "Incorrect! Try again."

Runt blinked twice. What did he mean?

"You've been out in the *world*," Mitch insisted. "You have to have discovered a new planet, or found buried treasure, or *something*. Now give!"

Runt's mind scrambled backward. "Noah said to tell you," he stammered, "that you're a royal pain in the behind."

Mitch laughed. "He's right. I am!"

Runt gave Mitch an uncertain smile.

"But that's not *new,* so it doesn't count." Mitch folded his arms. "One more chance."

Runt felt the way he did in school when he'd been called on and hadn't read the assignment. He hadn't talked to anyone besides Noah. What else could he say?

"Ticktock! Ticktock!" Mitch looked at his watch. "Ten seconds!"

"The trees!" Runt sputtered. "They've all changed!"

There were several seconds of silence and Runt's cheeks grew warm again. Why hadn't he said something else? Something that wasn't so dumb?

"Ping! A decent answer at last." Mitch grinned. "There's hope for you, Robert!" The grin faded. "May is my favorite time of year, and the beanbag's making me miss it."

Runt squinted at the edge of the bed. Was Mitch supposed to be making sense?

"All right." Mitch sighed. "I'll tell you what's going on, and then you pretend we never had this conversation, OK?"

Runt swallowed hard. He didn't think he was going to like what he was about to hear.

"I have cancer," Mitch said quietly. "I've had it for four years. It's not contagious, and you can't get it by being near me." He looked down at his hands. "So you don't have to freak out if I sneeze or something."

Runt nodded his understanding.

"The doctors have tried all the usual stuff for my kind of cancer, and none of it's worked. I go into remission for a month or two, and then the cancer comes back."

Runt winced.

"They're trying something experimental now." Mitch pulled up a sleeve to reveal a black-and-blue mark that began just above his wrist and disappeared into his pajama top. "A new kind of chemotherapy." He let his sleeve fall. "The IV needle's the size of a hockey stick."

Runt drew his breath through his teeth.

"Yeah," Mitch agreed. "And the needle's the easy part. The side effects are where you find the real laughs." He pointed to his bloated face. "My personal favorites are looking like a water balloon and feeling like I'm going to throw up twenty-four hours a day."

"Did the medicine?" Runt bit his lip. "Is that why your hair . . . ?"

Mitch nodded. "The chemo makes it fall out. The first time it happened, I dropped my hairbrush and screamed." He rubbed his head. "It was starting to come back, but now, with the new chemo . . ." He shrugged and raised one arm. "I used to look halfway decent."

Runt followed Mitch's outstretched hand to a photo on the dresser. A sturdy boy in a baseball uniform looked back at him with bright eyes. A thick shock of orange hair stuck out from under his cap. The rest of the figure looked nothing like the one in the bed, but the determined grin was unmistakably Mitch's.

"You played baseball?"

"*And* hockey, *and* football." Mitch snorted in disgust. "I also managed to get around without a wheelchair." His voice became high and sarcastic and sour. "And I went potty *all* by myself!"

Runt forced himself to look at Mitch.

"That's where the beanbag comes in." Mitch twisted a piece

of blanket between his hands. "When I first got sick, the doctors explained what was happening like it was some kind of battle." He closed his eyes. "The bad guys were the cancer cells. But with the help of the medicine, my white cells were going to wipe them out . . ."

His voice trailed off and Runt wondered whether he'd fallen asleep. A moment later, Mitch's eyes opened again.

"That story worked for a couple of years." He made a wry face. "But sometime during my *fourth* round of chemo, I decided that my body and I were two separate entities."

Runt's eyes widened.

"Inside, here and here . . ." Mitch pointed to his head and his heart. ". . . is where Mitch Curran lives." He raised his puffy arms and then let them fall. "The rest of my body is simply a beanbag."

Runt shifted restlessly.

"Beanbags don't have to worry about moving themselves from place to place. They don't care what they look like, and they don't feel pain."

Runt looked back to the photo on the dresser and whispered, "Are you going to die?"

"Of *course,* stupid!" Mitch snapped. "So are you!"

Runt caught his breath. That was true.

"Everyone has to die sometime!" Mitch's voice softened. "But I know what you meant. You were asking whether I'm going to die anytime *soon.*"

Runt slowly nodded.

"And the answer is, I don't know. Neither do the doctors." He shrugged and a faint grin appeared. "But you don't know, either. You could get run over by a car this afternoon, couldn't you?"

Runt nodded again.

"ok, then," Mitch said firmly. "That's settled. We're both going to die, and *neither one of us* knows when or how."

Runt suddenly felt dizzy.

"If we're going to be friends . . ." Mitch's eyes grew bright. ". . . we have to have gotten all that straight. I can't pal around with people who treat me like glass."

"I won't," Runt heard himself say.

"Good," Mitch growled. "Now go away!"

Runt's eyebrows shot up.

"Seriously," Mitch murmured. "I need to sleep. But come back on Monday, ok?"

"Noah's right." Runt grinned. "You *are* a pain in the behind!"

"But . . .?" Mitch held up one finger.

"But I'll come back on Monday."

Mitch closed his eyes. "See ya, Robert."

Runt met Mrs. Curran on the stairs.

"Oh!" Her face fell. "I was just bringing up a snack."

Runt looked at the tray in her hands. Lemonade and donuts!

"Mitch said he needs to sleep."

Mrs. Curran sighed. "I'm not surprised. It's been a bad week."

"I told him I'd come back on Monday."

Mrs. Curran smiled. "I'm glad. That'll give him something to look forward to." She tipped her head. "But don't you have school?"

Runt quickly shifted his gaze to the floor. "I'm visiting someone, so I'm not in school right now."

"I see. Then would you mind coming around noon? Mitch doesn't have much of an appetite, and he might eat more if you had lunch together."

Runt hesitated. He was already in deeper with Mitch than he'd ever intended to be. But how could he say no? Especially with Mitch's mother looking at him that way, the way Mary and Eve used to look when they wanted him to build something for them . . .

He took a deep breath and nodded.

"Wonderful." She led him down the stairs and set the tray on a table. "Let me give you our number, in case something comes up." She scribbled Curran and seven digits on a slip of paper and handed it to him. "What's your number, Robert?"

Runt lowered his eyes. The only phone in the trailer was Cole's cell phone, and he always kept that with him. "The place where I'm staying doesn't have a phone."

"Oh?" Mrs. Curran's eyes widened.

Runt shoved his feet into his sneakers. "But I'll call from a pay phone if I can't come."

"Thank you." Mrs. Curran quickly wrapped the donuts in a paper napkin. "The lemonade would be awkward to carry, but I hope you'll take these."

Runt clenched his teeth. Just because he didn't have a phone, that didn't make him a charity case.

"They'll only go to waste if you don't . . ."

Runt hesitated but finally accepted the package. "Thank you."

"Thank *you,* Robert. For coming." Mrs. Curran opened the front door and smiled again. "Have a good weekend!"

Runt nodded and hurried down the steps. The door snapped closed behind him and he slowed his pace. What was he running from, for Pete's sake? A woman who smiled a lot, and a kid with cancer . . .

Runt watched his shadow move ahead of him as he walked. How could Mitch have been sick for four whole *years?* Didn't cancer kill people quickly? And how could he cope with doctors, and needles, and wheelchairs—with having his whole body change—and still have a sense of humor?

13

Early evenings in the trailer were not pleasant.
Most of the time, Cole pointedly ignored Runt's presence. But he continued to boss and insult Helen, and Runt's loathing of him increased with each passing day. Although they seemed to make Helen happy, Runt didn't think dinner in a restaurant or a bouquet of flowers could compensate for the way Cole acted most of the time.

One evening, Cole demanded to know why supper wasn't ready. Did she think he wanted to eat in the middle of the *night,* for God's sake?

"Sorry, Cole," Helen said quickly. "The peas just need another minute."

Runt clenched his teeth. He'd taken over shopping for groceries and doing the laundry, but Helen was still on her feet all day, and she insisted on doing the cooking. And Cole never lifted a finger to help. Never said thank you, or even that the food tasted good . . .

The cell phone trilled and Cole flipped it open. "Yeah?" His eyes narrowed. "When?" He checked his watch. "I'll be there." He snapped the phone closed and shoved it into his pocket. "So much for dinner!"

He slammed through the door and the truck roared away. Helen gave the peas a final listless stir and turned off the stove. "C'mon, Runt. Bring your plate."

"Why d'you let him *talk* to you like that?" Runt sputtered. "How were you supposed to know his stupid phone would ring?"

Helen's back stiffened. "That's just Cole's way."

"Well, you deserve better!"

"Cole's good to me," she insisted. "Takes me places, buys me things."

"Yeah," Runt retorted. "Waving fifty-dollar bills around, like he's something rich." He folded his arms. "What's he even *do,* anyway?"

"What's he . . . ?"

"What's his *job?*"

A faint blush appeared on Helen's cheeks. "I'm not sure, exactly. He doesn't talk about work. Something to do with cars." She shrugged. "Get yourself some milk, all right?"

They ate in painful silence. Runt shoved bite after bite into his mouth, barely stopping to chew.

"C'mon, now," Helen finally said. "Let's not fight."

Runt's sigh stuck in his chest. Helen shouldn't have to put up with Cole, but saying so would only make her feel worse.

"Finish up," Helen said. "I've got something to show you."

Runt gulped the last of his milk, carried his dishes to the sink, and sat down again. Helen pulled an envelope from her pocket and set it on the table in front of him.

"Go on," she urged. "Have a look."

Runt picked up the envelope by one corner, and half a dozen photographs spilled onto the table. His eyes grew wide. "Where'd these come from?"

"I took them when I left." Helen's voice broke. "I had to have *something.*"

Runt reached for a photo of two smiling children, a girl who was eight or nine, and a toddler. "You and me?" he whispered.

"Yeah." Helen smiled. "Pretty cute, weren't you?"

Runt continued to stare. He remembered the dress Helen had on in the picture.

"Look at this one." She pointed to a snapshot of a barefoot six-year-old holding a fish nearly half his height. "Remember the day you caught that?"

"Nearly pulled the fishing pole out of my hand!" He grinned. "You had to help me reel it in."

"Had to get it off the hook, too," Helen said dryly. "And threaten you before you'd hold still so I could take the picture."

"Biggest I ever caught . . ." Runt took another look and set the photo to one side of the pile.

"That's all of us, on Eve's first birthday. And that's Mercy, just starting to walk . . ."

Runt's eyes began to water.

". . . and that one's Hope."

Runt tried to swallow and couldn't. There, in front of him, was the Hope he hadn't been able to call to mind. Her smile, her rosebud nose, her tiny fingers reaching up to grasp his . . . The picture suddenly blurred and he closed his eyes.

"I know," Helen said softly. "That's just how she was, ain't it? Here. Have a tissue."

Runt looked up. Helen's cheeks were wet, too. He blew his nose and wiped his eyes with the backs of his hands. He glanced at Hope's picture once more and reluctantly set it aside. He picked up the last photo and wrinkled his nose. Helen must have been about eleven, and he was probably five. But who was the woman with them, and what was behind them?

"Where was this?"

"Where we had that cookout you remembered. That's Ma's friend, Mrs. Miller. Her husband took the picture."

"What's that?" Runt pointed.

"The totem pole near the lake. Came all the way from British Columbia." Helen grinned. "You had bad dreams about it!"

Runt sat very still. He'd had nightmares about the carved fish on the pole. It was black and red, with concentric circles for eyes. "Why isn't Laura in the picture?"

"She wasn't there, remember?" Helen shook her head. "You were probably too little."

"I remember she wasn't, but not why."

"She got invited to go along on a friend's family vacation." Helen's eyebrows drew together. "I guess Ma felt sorry for us that time, being left behind. Mrs. Miller asked us to visit every summer, but that was the only time we went."

Runt squinted into the distance. "Their house was big, wasn't it?"

"Three stories. First floor was a restaurant. There were rooms for rent on the second, and they lived on top." She smiled. "I remember thinking it was real funny, having two kitchens in one house."

"Yeah. And the one upstairs had striped wallpaper."

Helen's eyes widened. "Imagine you remembering that!"

Runt grinned. "And Mr. Miller had a moustache!"

"Looked like a caterpillar."

Runt had thought the very same thing. They were just about to leave, and Runt was already in the back seat of the Chevy.

Mr. Miller leaned down to the window, and the little caterpillar wiggled above his smile.

"You remember, Robert. You and Helen can come stay with us anytime!"

Helen had heard him, too, and they'd laughed about it later. If Laura had been with them, they'd decided, Mr. Miller might not have issued such an open-ended invitation . . .

The door to the trailer slammed open. "Is supper ready *now*," Cole growled, "or do I get to eat it for breakfast?"

Helen rapidly scooped the pictures into the envelope. "I'll just heat it up for you."

Cole grunted and took a bottle of beer from the refrigerator. Runt watched him walk toward the far end of the trailer. He wondered whether, after eight years, the Millers' invitation might still be open.

He sighed crossly. Even if it was, how would he ever find the place? He didn't know their address, or the name of the town, or anything. He didn't even know their first names, for Pete's sake!

Helen carried Cole's dinner from the room and Runt flopped onto his bench. His connection with Helen had been broken as soon as Cole had returned. The memory of the Millers' invitation had lit a spark of hope that made his throat swell. Savagely, he crushed it.

14

Over the next several weeks, Runt settled into a routine. He left the trailer before Cole woke up and spent his mornings collecting cans and exploring the cemetery. At eleven thirty, his watch alarm would ring and he'd make his way to Peppertree Drive. He ate lunch at the Currans' house almost every day, skipping a visit only when Mitch had a doctor's appointment.

The rest of Mitch's wispy hair fell out, and his skin remained a pasty white, but his appetite slowly returned. The LCD television in Mitch's room had a DVD player attached to it, and they watched movies while they ate. Mitch had an impressive collection of videos. Runt was introduced to *Star Wars* and *Harry Potter* and *Finding Nemo,* and he saw film versions of classics he'd read: *The Secret Garden* and *The Chronicles of Narnia.* Each time he visited, he was able to stay a few minutes longer before Mitch announced that he needed to sleep.

One rainy day in early June Mrs. Curran opened the door with a grin that rivaled her son's best effort. "He's up!" She laughed. "He's in his chair!"

Runt's chest grew warm. "That's great!"

"You betcha!" Mrs. Curran laughed again. "He's feeling so good, he's going to . . ." She shook her head. "Nope. Can't steal his thunder."

Runt bit his lip. There wasn't *bad* news behind the good, was there?

"Go on up, Robert." Mrs. Curran tipped her head toward the stairs. "And give him as good as he dishes out!"

Runt pried off his sneakers and began to climb. His stomach flip-flopped when he reached the landing, and again just outside Mitch's door. He gently knocked twice.

"Enter!" Mitch's voice reverberated into a boom. "Robert the Bruce shows indecision to no one!"

Runt pushed open the door. Mitch was sitting in his wheelchair, facing the window.

"Hi."

Mitch spun the chair around. "And a porcine good morning to you!"

Runt stared, open-mouthed. Mitch was wearing a deadpan expression—and a rubber pig's snout.

"Or do you prefer a canine 'good day'?" Mitch replaced the pig snout with a dog's nose. "Or perhaps a reptilian greeting?" A pair of crocodile jaws appeared. "I rather like this one," Mitch admitted. "For encounters with The Cobra."

Runt grinned. "Those are great! Where'd you get them?"

"Mail order." Mitch wiggled his hairless eyebrows. *"Tons* of good stuff out there."

"A practical joker's heaven." Mrs. Curran stepped into the room. "Plastic dog poop, fake vomit, soap that turns your hands purple." She shook her head. "I wouldn't want to add up the money we've spent contributing to Mitch's delinquency."

"Geez, Mom. Why'd you spill the beans? I was about to offer Robert some gum."

Runt peered at the pack in Mitch's hand. Flavor Burst wasn't a brand he'd ever seen before.

"I wouldn't, if I were you, Robert," Mrs. Curran warned. "Not unless you're fond of chili peppers."

"No, thanks!"

Mrs. Curran checked her watch. "We have to leave in half an hour." She shot a questioning look in Mitch's direction.

"Haven't asked him yet." Mitch turned to Runt. "I've got ward duty this afternoon. Want to come?"

"What's ward duty?"

"Visiting kids in the hospital," Mitch said quickly. "Stirring up a little trouble and taking their minds off things."

"In other words," Mrs. Curran said, "Mitch would like you to be his partner in crime for the afternoon."

Mitch gave him a sly grin. "We're not *likely* to be arrested . . ."

Runt squinted at the floor. Was Mitch challenging him?

"We'll be back here by four." Mrs. Curran hesitated. "Sooner, if—"

"By four!" Patches of bright pink appeared on Mitch's cheeks.

"By four," his mother agreed. "Would that be too late, Robert?"

Runt shook his head.

"So," Mitch demanded, "you gonna come?"

Runt heard the plea behind the growl, and he nodded.

Mrs. Curran beamed. "Then I'd better get going on lunch!"

Her footsteps faded and Mitch gave Runt a conspiratorial wink. "She doesn't know the *half* of what I've got in here!" He lifted a small nylon bag from his lap. "We'll have some fun." He gazed out the window. "Thanks for saying you'd come. My mom could use some down time."

"Down time?"

"When I'm sick, she's on duty about twenty-three hours a day." Mitch cleared his throat. "If it's OK with you, I'll tell her to get lost this afternoon."

"Sure." Runt hesitated. "You'll show me what to do, right?"

Mitch nodded. "Step one is getting downstairs." He turned his wheelchair around. "Come on."

Runt followed Mitch to a narrow door at the end of the hall. Mitch pushed a button, the door slid open, and he backed his chair into an elevator a mere three feet square. "All aboard!"

Runt wedged himself into a corner. Mitch pushed another button, the door slid closed, and the elevator began its descent. It came to a stop with a very small bump.

"Not exactly *exciting*, as rides go," Mitch admitted. "But more convenient than stairs." He rolled into the kitchen. "The eagle has landed," he announced. "What's for lunch?"

"For Robert, real food." Mrs. Curran pointed to a sandwich roll piled high with tuna and lettuce. "For you, chocolate pudding and marbles. You want lemonade to wash them down?"

Mitch peered into a white bowl and sighed. "Can I have grape juice? The new brown ones are nasty."

"Sure." Mrs. Curran opened the refrigerator. "What would you like to drink, Robert?"

"Grape juice, please." He glanced sideways. Mitch's bowl contained dozens of tablets and capsules. A couple of them did look like marbles—big ones. "What *is* all that?" he whispered.

"My mother's latest attempt at gourmet cooking." Mitch made a face. "Vitamins. Minerals. Amino acids. Herbs."

Mrs. Curran winked at Robert. "And lizard's blood and bat wings!"

"Tastes like it," Mitch muttered.

"Sit down and eat, Robert," Mrs. Curran said briskly. "He'll whine all day if you give him an audience."

"True!" Mitch swallowed pills and grape juice in rapid succession. When the dish was empty, he burped very loudly and grinned. Runt couldn't help grinning back.

"Mitch!" Mrs. Curran glared at him.

"'Scuse me." Mitch grinned again.

Mrs. Curran handed him a bowl of chocolate pudding and a spoon and threatened to take away his bag of tricks if he didn't learn some manners. Mitch promised to behave, but when his mother left the room, he winked at Runt and burped again.

Mitch managed to control himself during the ride to the hospital, and when his mother lowered the wheelchair to the ground, he said tenderly, "It's a kid afternoon, Mom." He tipped his head. "Go to a movie or something, OK?"

"You sure?" She gave him a doubtful look. "You've only been out of bed for a few hours."

"I'm *fine.*" Mitch rolled forward. "And if I need anything, there are about six hundred doctors and nurses in there." He grinned over his shoulder. "Go away, Mom!"

"Meet you here at three thirty," she called.

Mitch waved, the automatic doors opened, and Runt followed the wheelchair into the lobby.

"*Mitch!*"

"Hey, Ebony!"

The nurse positively beamed as she hurried toward them. "How ya *doin'*, Trouble?" She leaned down to give him a hug.

"It's been dull as mud around here!"

Mitch nodded. "Figured it was time for a visit."

Ebony turned to smile at Runt. "And who is this? You bringing reinforcements now?"

"Double the trouble, double the fun!" Mitch said brightly. "My friend Robert."

Ebony held out her hand. "Pleased to meet you."

Runt took it. "You, too."

More shrieks brought more greetings, more embraces, more introductions. The process continued all the way to the elevator, and by the time the doors closed, Runt was dizzy.

"You know *everybody* in this place?"

Mitch shrugged. "You spend time somewhere, you make friends, right?"

The doors opened onto the sixth floor.

"Hey, look, everybody!" A bald little boy hollered. *"Mitch* is here!"

"Hey, Joey!" Mitch called back. "Got any new jokes for me?"

People swarmed toward the wheelchair from every direction —children, nurses, orderlies, people wheeling food carts, and teenagers whose nametags read Volunteer. Runt backed away from the crowd and surveyed his surroundings.

The sign above the nurses' station said Pediatric Oncology. Runt knew pediatric meant kids; oncology must mean cancer. He shook his head. He'd have expected a place for cancer patients to be depressing and quiet. This place was neither. It was immaculately clean and well lit, there were brightly colored posters on the walls, and the throng gathered around Mitch was making every bit as much noise as kids at recess.

"Hey, Mitch!" a deep voice said. "Move it into the playroom, will you? We've got to get down to radiology." An orderly nudged a gurney forward. On it lay a brown-skinned little girl whose hair was neatly braided and held in place by pink barrettes. Her wide brown eyes glistened with tears.

"Sorry about that, Tony!" Mitch spun his chair around. "Hang on a sec, will ya?"

Tony groaned. "You know how the rads are about schedules!"

"Thirty seconds won't kill 'em." Mitch rolled up to the gurney and smiled. "You're new, aren't you?"

The little girl nodded.

"My name's Mitch. What's yours?"

"Cindy." Her voice trembled. "Cynthia Jeanne DuBois."

"That's pretty." Mitch grinned. "Just like you!"

Cindy gave him a tiny smile.

"This your first time to radiation?"

She nodded.

"You know it doesn't *hurt,* right?"

Her chin quivered. "Promise?"

Mitch held up his right hand. "Promise. You just have to lie real still."

"OK."

Mitch reached into his bag, slipped something into her hand, and leaned close to her ear. When he sat up again, Cindy was smiling.

"Don't forget now!" He winked. "We've got a date next time I'm here." Mitch backed his chair away from the gurney. "OK, Tony. Thanks."

"Sure thing, Mitch."

The elevator doors closed with a hiss, and Mitch turned to a girl whose dirty blonde hair hung limply from among patches of pink scalp.

"Batista? You're looking a little ratty on top!"

Runt drew his breath through his teeth. How could Mitch have *said* that to the poor girl?

Batista stuck out her tongue. "Better'n you, Mitch!" She giggled. "You got ten, eleven hairs left up there?"

"You kidding?" He rubbed his head. "I look great. Grows back, I'm gonna start *shaving* it off!"

15

Mrs. Curran glanced into the rearview mirror.
"Is he asleep?"

Runt looked over his shoulder. Mitch's head drooped to one side. He was snoring softly, and a little bubble of spit twitched in one corner of his mouth.

"Sound asleep."

Mrs. Curran sighed. "I probably shouldn't have let him go today, but it was so good having him *want* to that I couldn't bring myself to say no."

"I think he liked seeing his friends," Runt said. "And everyone sure was glad to see him."

Mrs. Curran smiled.

"There was this one little girl," Runt stammered on, "who looked really scared. Mitch never even met her before, but he got her to smile."

"He has that effect on people . . ."

Runt nodded.

"Robert?" Mrs. Curran's voice shook a little. "Do you happen to know if anyone told him about Trevor?"

Runt's eyebrows drew together as he tried to remember.

Finally, he shook his head. "I wasn't next to him the whole time, but I didn't hear anyone say that name. Who's Trevor?"

Mrs. Curran glanced into the rearview mirror again. "A really *super* little kid." Her voice became husky. "One of Mitch's favorites." She turned into the driveway and switched off the engine. "He died last week."

Runt looked back at Mitch with alarm. He wouldn't have been so cheerful all afternoon if someone had told him. He must not know.

"Mitch was too sick to go to the funeral, so I put off telling him."

Runt winced.

"I'll *have* to tell him, and soon. But he's only just beginning to feel better himself, and he's going to take it hard."

Runt looked out the side window. "Has he lost other friends?"

"Trevor's the fourth."

Runt's chest contracted. He felt a desperate need to get out of the van, to put distance between himself and the Currans, but he couldn't make himself move.

"But he's got twenty *times* that number of friends in remission," Mrs. Curran added quickly. "Kids who are leading normal lives again."

Runt wasn't sure he'd heard correctly. There were kids with cancer who had really been cured? Lots and *lots* of them?

"Thanks for going with him today." Mrs. Curran gave him a brief smile. "It meant a lot to Mitch. And to me."

Runt focused his eyes on his sneakers. He didn't like the way his stomach felt, and he didn't know what to say. "You're welcome," he managed to mumble. "I'd better get going." He gave Mrs. Curran a quick nod and opened the door.

"Good night, Robert."

He raised a brief hand and began to walk quickly. Just before he rounded the corner, he glanced back. Mrs. Curran's arms were folded across the steering wheel and her forehead was resting on them.

16

"But Cole . . . !"

The wail rose and sailed past three trailers. Hairs rose on the back of Runt's neck. He held his breath and strained hard, but heard nothing more. His sneakers dug into graveled dirt and hurtled forward.

Bang!

The trailer's door bounced on its hinges and Runt jerked to a halt. Wild-eyed and flushed, Cole leaped from the top step to the ground. His black shirt was a blur as he stormed to the driver's door of the truck and slammed it behind him. The engine emitted a high-pitched whine and in seconds the truck was gone.

The cloud of dust began to drift, and Runt raced toward the trailer.

"Helen?" The kitchen was empty. "Helen!"

"In here."

Helen was standing in the living room, holding one hand to her cheek. Her shoulders were heaving and her eyes were bright with tears. Runt hurried toward her and she took a step back.

"You all right?"

"Yeah," she whispered. "I'm all right."

"What'd he *do* to you?" Runt demanded.

Helen took a long, shuddering breath and edged past him. "Leave it, Runt." Her voice cracked. "Just *leave* it, all right?"

The bathroom door closed with its small, tinny click.

RUNT SPENT TWENTY MINUTES KEEPING ONE EYE ON THE DOOR to the outside and both ears tuned to any sound from the bathroom. His vigil yielded nothing. Fuming and terrified, he finally retreated to his bench.

Cole had hit Helen—that much was clear. But *why?*

And why had she told him to "leave it" in a tone he'd never heard her use before? A voice that was flat, and hard, and designed to push him away.

Soundlessly, the bathroom door opened. A slight redness remained on one cheek, but Helen's eyes were dry.

"How was your day?"

Runt's jaw dropped. What was Helen trying to *do*, for Pete's sake? Pretend nothing had happened?

"What do you want for supper?" She crossed the room to the refrigerator.

Runt glared at her back. "Nothing!"

"All right." Helen shrugged. Without looking at him, she walked to the far end of the trailer.

Runt's disbelief faded, and his fear became a hot fury. Not just at Cole and what he'd done, but also at Helen, for refusing to acknowledge that it had happened. He shoved himself to his feet. Helen was lying on the sofa, facing the wall. He stopped in the doorway.

"That the first time he hit you?"

Several long seconds passed. "I told you to leave it, Runt."

"I'm not supposed to talk about the fact that he *hit* you?" Runt hollered. "I'm not supposed to worry that he'll do it again?"

"He only slapped me." Helen's voice was muffled by a pillow and her hair. "Not that hard."

Runt tried to fight down the rage that was pounding its way into his ears. His chest heaved with the effort. "He HIT you!"

In a single move, Helen pushed herself onto one hip and swung around to face him. Her eyes were cold. "You listen now, Runt. Stay out of this. It's between me and Cole."

Runt looked wildly around the room, struggling first to find words, and then his voice. "I am NOT just going to . . ."

"Yes, you ARE." Helen stood up. Her legs were shaking, but her eyes were even colder than they'd been a moment ago. "Unless you want to make things worse."

17

The moment Helen said that he might make things worse, Runt retreated—physically to his bench, and mentally inside himself.

It felt as though there were little devils inside of him, poking him everywhere with tridents. He couldn't think about Cole hitting Helen, and he couldn't *not* think about it. He tried, without success, to distract himself with a handheld video game that Mitch had given him.

Helen spent the evening watching TV. At nine thirty she said, "G'night," and the light in the living room went off. Cole returned very late, reeking of smoke and beer, and went to the front of the trailer without so much as a glance in Runt's direction.

The following morning, Helen continued to pretend nothing had happened, and Runt answered her few questions in a stilted but civil tone. When he got home that afternoon, Helen was wearing a necklace, a fine silver chain. She blushed when she saw that he'd noticed it, but she didn't say anything. It was a handsome present, Runt had to admit, and it looked lovely on her. But that didn't change what had happened.

Since his existence clearly annoyed Cole, Runt began to spend as little time as possible in the trailer. He devoted his days to scavenging roadsides for redeemable cans, and proudly watched his savings pass the sixty-dollar mark.

The rest of the time he explored the cemetery and delighted in the changes in the plants and trees around him. There was something very reassuring, something wonderfully predictable, in the way that the bright greens of early summer were edging their way toward the hot, dry greens of July.

He went to Mitch's house every weekday at noon. Several times, Mrs. Curran greeted him warmly but reported that Mitch was asleep.

On the last day of June, he found the driveway empty and a hastily written note taped to the door: Mrs. Curran was terribly sorry, but it had slipped her mind; Mitch had a doctor's appointment.

Runt spent a restless afternoon in the cemetery and decided to go back to the trailer early. He was relieved to find the truck missing from its accustomed place but disturbed to see a light shining from the front window. Helen should still be at work . . .

He opened the door and took a quick look around. On his bench sat a pile of magazines that hadn't been there when he left. Helen was lying on the sofa, still wearing her uniform. Her eyes were closed and a box of tissues lay on the floor. He tiptoed forward and knelt down.

"Helen?"

She opened her eyes.

"You ok?"

"Felt bad this morning, but I'm better now."

Runt shook his head. "You're sick."

"Mostly just tired," Helen protested, but her eyes closed again.

Runt decided that letting her sleep was the best thing he could do. Later, he'd heat up some soup and see if he could coax her to eat.

He returned to his bench and the magazines. Helen had been sick enough to leave work, but she'd bothered to bring him something to read? He picked up the stack and flipped through it. A copy of *Reader's Digest,* two issues of *National Geographic,* and a travel quarterly. He put everything but the travel magazine inside his bench, flopped onto his stomach, and started to read.

Twenty minutes later, he turned a page and stopped cold. In an advertisement for tourism in British Columbia, there was a photograph of a totem pole. The third carving from the bottom was a fish—a fish with concentric circles for eyes.

No, it wasn't the totem pole near the house by the lake, but it reminded him of that picture, and of Mr. Miller saying that he and Helen were welcome anytime. Even if they only visited for a day or two, it would get Helen away from Cole long enough to come up with another plan, another place to live . . .

He tossed the magazine onto the floor and swore. Right. Find the Millers (next to impossible), convince Helen to go (completely impossible), and arrange transportation (more impossible still).

He sank from depression into sleep. His nap ended when a pan banged onto the stove. He looked up to find Helen opening a family-size can of vegetable soup. She offered him a wan smile. "Both of us tired, huh?"

Runt rubbed his eyes. "How do you feel?"

"Tons better," Helen said quickly. "Fine now."

Runt was in no way convinced that Helen was fine, but there was no point in arguing.

HE CHANGED HIS MIND THE NEXT MORNING WHEN HE awakened to the unmistakable sounds of someone vomiting. He noted that Cole was still in bed and tiptoed to the bathroom door.

"Helen?" he whispered sharply.

"I'll be out in a minute." Her voice was hoarse.

It was a full eleven minutes later, and the toilet had flushed twice, before the door opened. Helen's cheeks were damp and the hair around her face was wet. She bit her lip and looked to her right. Cole hadn't moved, and she turned back to Runt.

"What're you doing up so early?"

"What's wrong?" he demanded.

"Touch of flu," she said wearily. "I'll be all right." She glanced at the clock on the stove. "I'd best get going."

"You crazy?" Runt's voice rose. "You were *throwing up* a minute ago!"

"Hush!" Helen stole another nervous glance at Cole. That was another one of his hang-ups: he didn't acknowledge, and certainly had no sympathy for, illness of any kind. "I'm fine now. Go on back to sleep."

Runt set his jaw. "I'm walking with you."

Helen opened her mouth to protest, closed it, and shrugged. "All right. Take something to eat."

Runt pocketed two pieces of bread and a slice of cheese and followed his sister down the steps. Neither of them spoke until they reached the restaurant.

"Thanks for the company."

Runt's eyes darted over Helen's face. "You all right to be on your feet all day?"

She nodded. "And I'll sit when I can." She gave his shoulder a quick squeeze. "Promise."

~

"ROBERT!" MRS. CURRAN OPENED THE DOOR THE REST OF THE way. "I'm so sorry about yesterday."

"That's OK," he said quickly. "How's Mitch doing?"

Her smile faded. "He's up. Out of bed, I mean."

Runt's eyebrows drew together.

"He's just sick of being sick today. Let him play a few practical jokes, and he'll be back to himself in no time." She gave him a reassuring smile. "I'll start some lunch."

The door to Mitch's room was open, but Runt knocked anyway. Mitch looked over his shoulder, nodded, and turned back to the computer screen. "I was hoping you'd show up."

Runt hesitated. Mitch didn't sound at all like himself.

Mitch waved a hand at the chair next to the desk. Runt watched the light from the computer screen flicker over Mitch's face. "What are you doing?"

"Surfing."

"What's that mean?"

Mitch stopped clicking and turned to stare at him. "You don't know what *surfing* is?"

Runt's face grew warm. "No."

Mitch sat back and gazed at Runt with an expression of open disbelief. "They don't have *computers* where you come from?"

Runt blushed again. "There were a few at school," he stammered. "But they didn't look like that." He pointed to the high-resolution screen. "They were just black with green words. And only the teachers got to use them."

"So you've never been on the net?"

"I know what a *net* is," Runt growled. "Just not a computer one."

Mitch suddenly grinned. "Well, today's your lucky day, Mr. Remick. Allow me to introduce you to the twenty-first century!"

Runt managed a small smile.

"So you know nothing about the Internet?"

Runt shook his head.

"ok." Mitch fixed his gaze on the ceiling. "You know how telephones work, right? And that if you dial extra numbers, you can call anywhere in the world?"

Runt nodded.

"Well, it's the same sort of thing. If you know someone's e-mail address—the telephone number for their computer—you can send them a message." A little arrow darted across the screen. "See?" He clicked. "Here's my address book."

Runt leaned forward to examine the box that popped open. There were a lot of funny names and numbers, most of them unpronounceable, each followed by "@" and more funny names, like hotmail.com and aussienet.com.

Mitch moved the arrow. "That's my friend Danny, that's The Cobra, that's Dad at work . . ."

"Like a telephone book!"

"Right. Only better, because it only has the people you want in it, and they can be anywhere." Mitch grinned. "I've got friends in Canada and Scotland and Australia—all over the place!"

Runt gave him a doubtful look. "How'd you meet them?"

"Chat rooms, mostly." Mitch began to click rapidly. "Here's one on football that I used to visit a lot when I was feeling . . . athletic."

Runt winced at the sarcasm in *athletic.*

"Here we go." Mitch clicked again and leaned back.

Next to more funny names, lines of type were appearing on the screen, one after another. An argument seemed to be under way about which quarterback should start in Chicago's first preseason game. Suddenly, this message appeared:

Hi, Mitch! Where've you been?

Mitch rapidly typed, "Hey, Tim. Gotta go. E-mail me, OK?" He clicked again, and a second later,

Hey, Tim. Gotta go. E-mail me, OK?

appeared on the screen. Mitch clicked once more, and the box disappeared. "Tim's a good kid," he explained. "But he can go on for hours about nothing."

Runt nodded his understanding about Tim and then shook his head at this whole new way of communicating.

"I've met a few idiots online," Mitch admitted. "But it's also how I met my two closest friends." He gave Runt a small smile. "Besides you, that is. Now, you want to see what else is out there? Pick a topic, ANY topic!"

"What do you mean?"

"I mean anything you want to know more about. I guarantee there's a Web site on it."

"What's a Web site?"

"Kind of like a little library. Here, let me show you." Mitch's fingers sped across the keyboard and a dinosaur came into view. "Interested in paleontology?" His fingers danced again, and Jupiter appeared. "Or is astronomy more your thing?"

Runt's temples began to pound as he thought of the invitation Mr. Miller had left open. "Can it find . . . totem poles?"

18

Mitch folded his arms. "You don't want much, do you?"

The call to lunch had come just as Runt posed his question. When they returned to the bedroom, Mitch wrung from him every meager detail he had about the Millers.

"I'm sorry," Runt pleaded. "But that's all I can remember. I was only five."

"Can't you at least get the photo to work from?"

Runt shook his head. "I don't know where Helen keeps it, and I don't want her to know I'm trying to find them."

"Why not?" Mitch demanded. "There's nothing criminal about looking up an address."

A sudden urge came over Runt—a desperate desire to tell Mitch about Ma and Helen and Cole and all of it. To make him see how truly important it was that he find the Millers. He glanced up, saw the exhausted pallor in Mitch's face, and swallowed hard. "I just can't, OK?"

Mitch sighed and reached for a pen. "All right. We'll do what we can. What's the name of the place you're from again?"

"Farnham."

He spelled it and Mitch scribbled the name. "Now *think*, Robert. Pretend you're five again."

Runt nodded.

"You're getting into the car to go to the Millers'. What did it look like outside?"

Runt gave him a puzzled look. "Like home. Like always."

"Not that!" Mitch snapped. "What time of day was it?" His voice grew softer. "What was the light like?"

"Early," Runt said eagerly. "Real early. The sunshine was bright, but the shadows were still really long, and the trees were mostly just outlines!"

Mitch grunted. "Good. And it was summertime, right? Let's guess it was six or six thirty. Something like that. Now think again. What was the light like when you got there?"

"Close to noon," Runt said promptly. "We got to go swimming for a little while, and then we had the barbecue."

"Mitch?" Mrs. Curran called from the hall. "Ten more minutes, and then a nap."

Mitch glowered at the door and turned back to Runt. "So you were in the car about six hours. Did you stop much?"

Runt shook his head. "Maybe once for gas. But it was pretty much all dirt roads. No highways, so we couldn't have been going very fast."

Mitch nodded his approval. "Thirty, maybe forty miles an hour. Max." He turned back to the computer, typed and clicked, and in less than a minute, a map appeared with a star in the center next to the word *Farnham*.

"Forty times six." Mitch resumed clicking. "Two-hundred-and-forty-mile radius."

The map jumped in size. Farnham remained in the center, but the map now included nearby towns. Mitch checked the scale at the bottom of the map and clicked twice more. Reference points for Farnham now included three major cities and two state lines.

Runt grinned. "You did it!"

"Hmmmph!" Mitch sounded exactly like Noah. "Don't send out the party invitations just yet. All we've done is narrow the search from the continental u.s. to an area the size of Maryland."

"So what do we do now?" Runt asked.

Mitch began to shut down the computer. "*You* try to remember anything else you can about the place, or how you got there." The screen went dark. "And *I* get some rest."

"ok." Runt was alarmed to find that Mitch's eyes had closed. "You want help getting into bed or anything?"

Mitch shook his head. "My mom'll do it."

"Thanks a lot." Mrs. Curran's footsteps came toward the door. "See you."

Runt assured Mrs. Curran that he could let himself out. He eased the front door closed, heard the lock click, and checked his watch. An hour and a half until Helen got off work. Enough time for a quick visit to the cemetery.

NOAH SPIED RUNT COMING THROUGH THE GATE AND CAME toward him. His limbs didn't jerk quite so much when he moved slowly.

"Seen him lately?" Noah examined Runt with wary eyes.

"Just now."

"How's he doing?"

"He's awfully pale," Runt admitted. "And tired."

Noah gave him a piercing look. "How tired?"

"He was going to take a nap when I left."

"Play any tricks on you today?" Noah demanded.

Runt shook his head. "Just did some stuff on his computer."

Noah squinted into the distance, and for the first time since Runt had met him, his eyebrows remained still.

"Tell him from me," he finally growled, "to get himself over here one of these days. Got things to show him."

"I'll tell him."

Noah squinted again, this time directly at Runt. "Stay with him now, Robert."

Before Runt could react, Noah turned and began walking away at such a rapid pace that Runt wondered how his jerking limbs managed to stay attached to his body.

The whole way into town, he wondered what Noah had meant. Not the words, but what had made Noah say them.

By ten minutes to four, Runt was stationed across the street and two blocks from Hayden's. He heaved a sigh of relief when Helen came down the steps: at least she hadn't been sick enough to leave in the middle of the day. Runt ducked behind a truck and ran toward the main road. He didn't want Helen to know he'd been spying on her.

HE WAS RUMMAGING IN A CUPBOARD FOR A BOX OF MACARONI when Helen arrived. She still didn't look right, Runt decided, but she looked better than she had this morning.

"How you feeling?" he asked.

"Hey, Runt." She gave him a wan smile. "What're you up to?"

"Fixing us supper."

"All right if I lie down for a while?"

"'Course," Runt said quickly. "Maybe you can sleep some."

Helen slept for an hour and a half. Between cooking tasks,

Runt tried to remember more about their visit with the Millers. He recalled how cold the lake water had been, and how good the hamburgers had tasted, but nothing that might help identify the location of the totem pole.

When Helen woke up, she complimented Runt on his macaroni salad but ate next to nothing. She said Cole would be gone until tomorrow night and suggested watching TV. They settled on a comedy about a family vacation, and Runt hoped he could bring up their trip to the Millers without arousing Helen's suspicion.

The movie family piled into a station wagon and Runt was about to broach the subject when Helen announced that she really needed to go to bed.

Crushed, Runt turned off the TV.

HE HAD HORRENDOUS NIGHTMARES THAT NIGHT. ONCE AGAIN he dreamed that he and Helen were in the woods back home, that she was calling to him and he couldn't find her. Only this time, he knew she was badly hurt.

And he dreamed that he was alone and hungry back in Farnham. The town landmarks were familiar, but all of the people were strangers. When he tried to buy something to eat, the strangers who were running the Winters' store refused to take his money.

He awakened just before dawn from a dream that had terrified him. The only thing he could recall was that Mrs. Miller had called her husband Quinn.

~

"WELL, THAT'S SOMETHING," MITCH GRUNTED LATER THAT morning. "I'd hate to think how many John Millers and James

Millers are out there." He reached for the mouse and turned back to Runt. "What's wrong with you?"

Runt scowled. "Nothing."

Mitch gave him a piercing look from under his lashless eyelids. "Bull," he said quietly. "But I'm not going to pry." He shrugged very slightly. "I know what it's like not to want to talk, and then to have people keep hammering at you."

"What are you getting hammered about?"

"How I *feel.*" Mitch's voice was filled with disgust.

"Like, 'Are you going to throw up?'"

Mitch shook his head. "Not the physical stuff. Emotional." He folded his arms and lifted his chin. "Like how I feel about the fact that this latest round of chemo hasn't done *jack.*"

Runt swallowed hard. "It hasn't helped?"

"Not one stinking bit," Mitch snarled. "The beanbag's been puking its guts out for nothing. The cancer's still having a field day."

Runt winced. "So what happens now?"

"I have to decide whether to keep trying or not." He looked at Runt with an odd mixture of resignation and defiance. "Whether to do another round of chemo and hope for some sort of god-damn miracle . . ."

Runt's breath stuck in his throat.

". . . or try to actually *enjoy* the time I have left."

19

The enormity of the decision Mitch was facing,
and the casual way he'd described it, set every nerve ending
in Runt's body on fire. His unfocused eyes saw only a reddish
brown haze, and the buzzing in his ears drowned Mitch's voice.

"Robert?" Mitch leaned forward and sharply nudged his arm.
"You still *in* there?"

The haze and the buzzing began to fade.

"You all right?"

It was the last thing Runt wanted to do, but he forced himself
to look directly at Mitch.

"Yeah," Runt whispered. "Sorry," he added in a slightly
stronger voice.

Mitch shrugged. "'S ok. Lots of people don't like to talk
about death." He jerked a thumb at the computer. "Remember
my two other best friends? The ones I know only online?"

Runt looked at the computer and nodded.

"They've got cancer, like me." Mitch gave another small
shrug. "We're close because we share things no one else wants to
talk about."

"Like dying."

Mitch nodded. "And treatments. And how our parents are doing. And whether or not God exists." He hesitated. "And how it feels to lose real-time friends who can't handle how much we've changed . . . and can't handle not knowing what will happen next."

He turned his head and shrank into the curving leather of his wheelchair. Time stood still again, but now Runt was conscious of it.

"Please?"

A very small sound. Had Runt heard it, or only imagined it?

He looked at Mitch. And saw—with bone-chilling clarity—Mitch's few strands of new hair, the whiteness of his skin, the hollows above his swollen cheeks.

Runt shuddered, and then a calmness settled over him, one that left him certain that he was making the right decision.

"Mitch?" he ventured.

His eyes opened abruptly. "Yeah?"

Mitch's voice was filled with anger—pretend or real? Runt wasn't sure.

"Nice that you've finally learned my name." Mitch examined him with wary, watery eyes. "How come it took talking about dying to get you to say it?"

Runt's cheeks tightened against an unwanted smile. "I'm slow, all right?"

Some of the tension went out of Mitch's shoulders. "Sure are."

Runt took a deep breath. "Whatever you decide," he said in a low, clear voice, one he wouldn't have recognized in a million years as his own, "we'll still be friends."

Mitch's cheeks took on a momentary blush.

"For keeps," Runt added, not knowing where that had come from.

Mitch's eyes remained closed, but his lips curled into a small smile. "For someone who's a total jerk, you're OK."

Runt looked at Mitch's translucent skin and hesitated. Then he reached out and gently punched his shoulder. "For someone who's a lunatic, so are you."

"ROBERT?"

Runt released his grip on the handle of the Currans' front door. He'd hoped to sneak out without talking to Mrs. Curran. There was simply too much jostling around his insides to risk adding anything more.

"Are you all right?"

Runt felt blood rush to his cheeks.

"Did you and Mitch talk . . . ?"

Runt knew that if she finished that sentence, his chest would explode. "He's asleep!" he nearly shouted.

"All right," Mrs. Curran said quietly. "I won't ask about Mitch. But I want to ask you something else."

Runt bit his lip.

"You never mention your family, or other friends." Mrs. Curran's forehead became furrowed. "Do you have anyone you can talk to?"

"Never been much for talking."

Mrs. Curran smiled very briefly and resumed looking at him with worried eyes. "We all need someone to listen." Her voice softened. "Especially when we're not sure what we're feeling."

Runt clenched his fists.

Mrs. Curran's voice brightened, although it was clear that she was making an effort. "You still haven't met Mitch's dad, have you?"

Runt shook his head.

"Tell you what, then." Mrs. Curran gave him another quick smile. "You check at home, and if it's all right, we'll have you to dinner one night next week."

Runt managed a single bob of his head, as though dinner next week sounded like a good idea.

"Thanks." He pulled open the door. "See you tomorrow."

RUNT BROKE INTO A TROT ON THE CURRANS' FRONT LAWN AND loped past the cemetery. When he reached the main road, he fixed his eyes on the horizon and hurtled toward it. He ran without thinking, desperate to find solace in the pounding of his feet and lungs.

On and on he ran, drawing in gasps of hot, dusty air, oblivious to the world around him. When at last he stopped, it was only because he was forced to. Chest heaving, he watched a stream of freight cars rumble along the track that blocked his way. By the time the last car passed, his body refused to run any farther. With heavy steps, he began the long walk back to the trailer park.

Mitch hadn't said what he was going to do. He'd only said that he had a *decision* to make. Runt allowed himself a moment's hope that Mitch would choose to continue treatment, that somehow a "goddamn miracle" *would* occur. But then he recalled a conversation they'd had shortly after Mitch's last chemotherapy session.

The hospital bed in Mitch's room had been nearly flat and his skin so white that Runt had to use shadows to determine where sheets left off and his friend began. A hideously colorful exception to the whiteness—Mitch's left arm—was a mass of angry purple bruises that spread out from a beige bandage. The urine bag was again hanging from its hook, and there was a plastic bowl on Mitch's pillow.

Runt forced himself to walk forward. "Hi," was all he could think of to say.

Mitch winced. "Hey."

"That arm hurt as bad as it looks?"

"Yeah, actually. It does." Mitch sighed very softly. "We're not exactly doing quality-of-life stuff today."

Runt's eyebrows drew together and Mitch gave him a weak smile.

"Zero energy . . . barf bowl . . . diapers . . . The Works."

Mitch closed his eyes and Runt held his breath—knowing, dreading the words his friend would speak next. Long minutes passed before Mitch roused himself and continued.

"When that's what you wake up to, dying doesn't look all that bad."

20

As Runt came up the road to the trailer park he
spied Cole's truck. He was four trailers away when he heard
Cole holler, "I don't want to hear another WORD about this!"

Runt raced forward, yanked open the door, and came to an
unsteady halt in the kitchen. Helen was sitting on the sofa, her
head in her hands. Cole was standing above her, red-faced and
fists clenched. Suddenly, he reached out and grabbed a handful
of her hair.

"You *hear* me, bitch?"

Without thinking, Runt launched himself at Cole. The last
thing he saw was the contempt in Cole's eyes.

"HONEYBEE?"

Someone, somewhere far away, was calling him. Runt wanted to answer but couldn't. A heavy blackness lay over him, and
it was holding the pain at bay.

"C'mon, now." The voice shook. "Wake up."

Runt forced his eyes open. The pain exploded, filling his
head, and he quickly shut them again. Someone groaned and
the throbbing doubled in intensity.

"That's it. C'mon now."

Several agony-filled eternities passed.

"Honeybee? Can you talk?"

Runt started to shake his head and fought down a wave of nausea.

"C'mon now. Try," Helen urged. "Say *something.*"

"Can't."

"Good, Runt. *Real* good." The words came out in a grateful sigh. "You know who I am?"

"Helen." Runt groaned again. "What happened?"

"You went after Cole," she said slowly. "He swung at you, and you hit your head on the table."

Runt's eyes darted everywhere as he struggled to rise. "Where is he?"

"Hush and lie still!" Helen said sharply. "He went out."

Twenty minutes later, Runt was propped up at the kitchen table holding one ice-filled towel to his left cheek and a second one to the back of his head. He felt sick to his stomach, but the throbbing had eased to the point where he could see clearly again.

Helen dumped a can of stew into a bowl, put it into the microwave, and looked out the window. "Runt?"

"Yeah?"

"I know you meant well. Trying to protect me and all . . ."

Runt's eyes narrowed.

". . . but don't you ever do anything like that again!"

Runt slammed both hands onto the table. Pieces of ice broke free of the towels and skittered in every direction.

"I'm just supposed to watch him treat you . . ." He choked. ". . . worse than a dog?"

"I mean it, Runt!" The color rose in Helen's cheeks. "You've probably got a *concussion* right now. And Cole said if you ever try to touch him again, you and me are out on the street!"

"Better than being with him!" Runt shouted back. The effort nearly blinded him with pain.

"You're dead wrong about that." Helen's voice was hard. "I've *been* on the street, and I know."

RUNT REFUSED TO EAT AND RETREATED TO HIS BENCH. HELEN was sitting alone at the table, listlessly stabbing at the remains of her stew, when the sound of Cole's truck came through the window. Runt sat up too quickly and had to steady himself with his hands. Helen shot him a warning glance and turned toward the door. Runt fastened his eyes on Cole's chest and cautiously shifted his weight to the balls of his feet.

"Didn't expect you back so soon," Helen said with a lightness Runt was certain she didn't feel. "I'll start something for your supper."

"You do that." Cole's voice was soft and full of menace.

Runt watched her begin to take things from the refrigerator. Helen was so clearly miserable that a part of him wished he could offer her comfort. Another part of him was still far too angry. That part grew even angrier as he watched the meticulous way she arranged Cole's dinner tray. Everything perfect, and all for someone who didn't remotely deserve it.

21

Runt lay motionless in the semidarkness, listening past the pounding in his temples for any sign that his sister was awake. He'd already taken inventory of his injuries: there was a large lump on the back of his head and dried blood matted into his hair. His cheek was swollen and painful to touch, and he could open his left eye only half way. But it was the ache in his chest that bothered him most.

The door to the far end of the trailer opened silently and closed again.

"Oh! Didn't know you were awake," Helen stammered. "How're you feeling?"

"How're YOU feeling?"

"Don't *be* like that, Runt!" she spat back. "I told you—this is between me and Cole."

THE BATHROOM DOOR CLOSED BEHIND HELEN, AND RUNT DOVE for his money and his jacket. She might have had the last *word,* but he was going to have the last *action.*

He was leaving.

It was the only thing he could think of that might get Helen away from Cole.

He reached the main road, turned left, crossed two lanes of traffic, and prepared himself to hitchhike back to Farnham.

He walked for two hours before a car finally slowed down. A teenager in a Red Sox baseball cap turned down the music coming from the radio and called, "Where you headed?"

"Farnham," Runt called back.

"Never heard of it," the teenager said. "But I'm going as far as Lockport."

Runt gratefully pulled open the passenger door.

"I'm Ryan," the driver announced as he pulled back onto the road. "And you would be?"

"Robert," stammered Runt. "And thanks a lot."

"So, what's in Farnham that makes it worth getting to?"

Runt groped for words, and finally shook his head.

"Then what was in Westfield that made it worth leaving?"

Runt's eyes began to sting. "My sister . . ."

"What about her?"

Before he knew it, Runt was pouring out his life's story. "I didn't know what else to do," he finally said, "to get her away from Cole."

"Did you *tell* her that's why you were leaving?"

Runt shook his head.

"So she's going to come home," Ryan's voice took on an edge, "and you're just not going to *be* there?"

Runt's cheeks grew warm. He'd taken off without thinking that far ahead.

"I hate to say it, Robert, but the only thing running away is going to accomplish is scaring the hell out of your sister." He pulled into a gas station and brought the car to a halt. "This is the turnoff for Lockport. Whatever you decide to do, good luck."

With weary dismay, Runt watched the car disappear. He suddenly knew Ryan was right, and he was almost fifteen miles from Westfield.

IT WAS JUST AFTER FIVE WHEN HE CLIMBED THE STEPS TO THE trailer. No one had offered him a ride on the way back, and his legs were trembling with exhaustion.

"You look beat!" Helen's brow became furrowed. "What you been up to today?"

"Nothing."

~

RAIN HAMMERED RUNT AS HE HURRIED THE LAST BLOCK TO the Currans', but he was long past noticing. He'd been soaked to the skin by the time he reached the main road. He was no longer aware of being cold, but he was very aware of the darkness around him. The clouds overhead were heavy and low, and it felt almost like dusk. He knocked twice and waited, fighting a sudden desire to go to sleep.

"Robert?" Through the partly open front door, Mrs. Curran examined him with wary eyes.

"Hi." Runt shifted uneasily from one foot to the other. Where was the welcoming smile he'd come to expect? "Is Mitch up to a visit?"

Mrs. Curran's eyes filled with tears. "He was devastated yesterday. No visit. No phone call." Her voice broke. "He thought you were gone for *good!*"

"I'm sorry," Runt pleaded, scrambling through his mind for an acceptable excuse. "My sister was sick. *Really* sick!"

The door opened the rest of the way. "Is she feeling better?"

"Some. Thanks."

"You're drenched!" Mrs. Curran's voice was suddenly filled with concern. "Stay here for a minute, and I'll get you something dry to put on."

She returned with a terry cloth bathrobe and pointed to a lavatory off the hall. "Leave your clothes on the sink and I'll throw them in the dryer." She raised a hand to his still swollen cheek. "That's a nasty cut, Robert. What happened?"

"I tripped." Runt's ears burned. "It's nothing."

Mrs. Curran crooked a finger under his chin and peered closer. "It's a 'nothing' that needed stitches." She shook her head. "I'd better let Mitch know you're here."

Runt stepped into the lavatory and closed the door. Two minutes later, clad only in damp underpants and the deliciously thick bathrobe, he climbed the stairs. Outside of Mitch's room, Mrs. Curran gave him a small smile. Runt breathed a quick sigh of relief and went in.

"Hey." Mitch was propped against a mountain of pillows, but his eyes looked alert.

"Hi." Runt took a few uncertain steps forward. "I'm sorry about yesterday. My sister was sick."

"Is she better?"

Runt nodded.

"How come you never talk about her? You never talk about *anyone* in your family."

Runt shrugged. "What do you want to know?"

Mitch waved one hand in a circle. "What about your parents? You got any other brothers or sisters?" He pointed to his desk chair. "Sit. I'm not going anywhere."

"Well . . ." Runt began, and then stopped. He'd never talked about his family and was forced to grope for words. "My Ma and Pa are both dead."

Mitch's expression did not change.

"Never had any brothers. Six sisters."

Mitch's eyes widened. "Six?"

Runt nodded. "Helen—the oldest—she's the one I live with." He took a deep breath. "Then comes Laura, then me. Then Mary and Eve." He swallowed hard. "Mercy and Hope were the youngest."

Mitch tipped his head to one side. "Were?"

"Yeah." Runt felt his chest tighten. "They both died."

"How?" Mitch said softly.

"Mercy drowned," Runt managed to croak, "when she was a year and a half." He looked at his hands. "Hope was just a baby. Crib death, Ma called it." He faltered, and then the words rushed forth. "I was the one who found her."

Mitch stared at him and then sighed. "Just proves how dumb it is to jump to conclusions."

Runt looked up.

"When you didn't show up yesterday, I thought you'd blown me off because you couldn't handle talking about death." He snorted softly. "And here it turns out you've lost four people in your immediate family. Guess you know something about death after all."

Runt shook his head. "I don't understand anything about it."

"Well, none of us does, really," Mitch admitted. "We can't. Not until we've gone through it." He tipped his head. "Do you believe in ghosts?"

Runt wrinkled his nose. "Ghosts?"

"Yeah. Haunted houses, and all that. People coming back from the dead to communicate with the living."

Runt shook his head.

"I do!" Mitch suddenly grinned. "And I'm planning on haunting up a storm!"

~

MRS. CURRAN RETURNED RUNT'S CLOTHES, FRESH FROM THE dryer, and insisted he drink an enormous mug of steaming soup. He headed for home thoroughly warmed but in a pensive mood. He didn't believe in ghosts—he *knew* he didn't—but he couldn't stop trying to imagine the sort of ghost Mitch might make. Considering what a practical joker he was in the flesh, what kinds of tricks might he pull if he were invisible and able to fly through walls?

The smell of something sweet brought Runt out of his reverie. He looked up to find himself in the cemetery and flowers blooming all around him. A moment later, he found himself looking down at a familiar headstone:

At Rest
Louisa Houck
died Jul. 19, 1874
AET 4 days

He remembered wondering, the first time he'd seen it, why little Louisa Houck had ever been born at all. Now he wondered if her ghost lived on . . .

Had Mitch been serious about believing in ghosts? Or had he

just been teasing? Runt poked a stick into the grass. Hard to tell with Mitch, sometimes. He grunted. Hard to tell with Mitch a *lot* of the time . . .

Or had the joke about ghosts been his way of telling Runt that he wasn't going to have any more treatments?

~

THE FOLLOWING MORNING, RUNT CLIMBED THE STEPS TO Mitch's room with butterflies in his stomach. He felt consumed with the need to ask but had no idea how he'd find the words. And, he admitted to himself, he was afraid of the answers.

Mitch was in his wheelchair, at the computer. By way of greeting, he handed Runt two pages filled with addresses.

"That'll be one hundred and twenty dollars, please!"

Runt's mouth dropped open.

"Thirty bucks an hour is *cheap,*" Mitch said with mock indignation. "Top-of-the-line researchers usually make four times that much!"

Runt caught the twinkle in his eye and looked down at the sheets. Each entry began, "Miller, Quinn."

"How did you get these?"

"Wasn't easy," Mitch admitted. "Had to find zip codes for every part of that map we came up with. Then I used three different search engines, and every address-locator site they had on each one."

Runt gave him a blank look.

"Never mind," Mitch said. "I'm pretty sure I got everything that's out there." He held up one hand in warning. "But no guarantee that the Miller you want is on the list. If they've moved outside of that circle, or they've got an unlisted number, you're out of luck."

Runt nodded his understanding and stammered, "Thanks a lot, Mitch."

"No problem." He turned back to the computer. "You can use our address, if you want."

"For what?"

"You'll have to put a return address on the letters, won't you?" Mitch demanded. "So they can write back? You said you didn't want your sister to know you're trying to find them."

Runt tucked the papers into his pocket. "Thanks." He hesitated and then blurted out, "Do you really believe in ghosts?"

Mitch laughed. "Well, if I do, I'm not alone." He typed rapidly and a page that said "Google" popped onto the screen. He entered "ghosts," hit return, and a list of Web sites appeared. Mitch pointed to the top of the page.

Results 1–10 of about 18,400,000.

"That means there are more than eighteen million Web pages about ghosts." He clicked some more and the screen went dark. "But to answer your question—no, I don't believe in ghosts. Not the kind you see in movies, anyway."

"Some other kind?"

Mitch gave him a thoughtful look. "More like a spirit. Something unique to each person that lives on after the body is gone."

"You've thought about this a lot," Runt said simply.

Mitch shrugged. "Kind of hard not to, given the circumstances." He gave Runt a sad smile. "One of the perks of having a lengthy and debilitating illness." He looked out the window. "The Cobra's coming this afternoon."

"Your doctor?"

Mitch nodded. "To discuss my options."

"You mean, more treatment . . ." Runt swallowed hard. "Or not."

Mitch nodded again, very slowly this time. "Unless she's got something really good up her sleeve, I think it's time to call hospice."

"What's hospice?"

Mitch's mouth twitched. "Scouting agents for the grim reaper."

"What?!"

"Kidding, Robert." Mitch gave him a very brief smile. "They're people who help you die. The way you want to die."

22

The wheelchair lift began its slow descent, and
Mitch's nose twitched. He breathed deeply, savoring the odors
of damp earth and summer roses.

"Oh, MAN, that smells good!"

Mrs. Curran and Runt grinned at each other. When the lift
quietly thumped to a halt, Mitch released the brakes on his chair
and rolled forward.

"C'mon, Robert. We've got places to go and things to see."

"How long, Mitch?" Mrs. Curran set the lift into motion
again. "Two hours?"

Mitch shook his head. "At least three."

"Three, then." Mrs. Curran glanced at her watch. "But no
more than that. Meet you back here." She slammed the door of
the van and gave them each a smile. "Enjoy yourselves."

"No problem!" Mitch turned to Runt. "Is this a perfect day,
or what?"

Runt looked around at patches of flowers in dappled sunlight.
"Never seen a better one." He glanced at the retreating van and
checked his own watch. "Where to?"

"Let's just wander for awhile first," Mitch said. "Feels like a hundred years since I've been outside, and I want to soak in as much of it as I can."

Mitch had been watching a movie when Runt arrived at the Currans' house that morning, and he insisted that Runt watch the end of it with him. There had been no mention of Dr. Colandra's visit, nor of any decisions that might have been made. During lunch, Mitch had announced his intention to spend the afternoon in the cemetery and had made it clear that Runt was to accompany him.

Runt ambled alongside the wheelchair in silence, pausing occasionally when Mitch stopped to admire some growing thing, or called out a greeting, as though to an old friend.

"Afternoon, Major!" Mitch offered an ornate gray headstone a smart salute. "Great day to be among the living!"

He dissolved into laughter, and Runt wondered whether it was at his joke, or at the bewilderment he knew was evident on his own face.

"Don't sweat it, Robert." Still chuckling, Mitch rolled forward again. "Never hurts to be friendly, dead or alive."

They had covered half a mile of winding paths before he spoke again. "You know any of your grandparents?"

Runt shook his head. "They all died before I was born." He hesitated. "How about you?"

"Just one." Mitch brought the chair to a halt. "My mother's mother. Nana." He smiled. "Nana-Banana, I used to call her."

Runt's eyes grew wide. "She didn't mind you calling her that?"

"Mind?" Mitch laughed. "She loved it! She loved me." Mitch looked into the distance. "I've always been glad that she died before I got sick."

Runt thought hard for a moment and then nodded.

"I missed her something fierce," Mitch whispered. "I still miss her." He began to tremble and his eyes filled with tears. "That's the only thing that really bothers me . . ."

His voice broke, and Runt watched in horror as tears flooded Mitch's cheeks. Heart pounding, Runt eased himself onto his knees next to the wheelchair. He sensed that Mitch needed him to be close, but he wasn't sure whether he wanted to be touched.

"What's the only thing?"

Mitch suddenly sobbed and held out his arms. Awkwardly, Runt leaned forward and wrapped his arms around Mitch's quaking torso. Mitch gripped him with a strength that Runt found terrifying, but he tightened his own grip in return. Mitch's chest began to heave and Runt desperately wished he weren't alone with him, wished he had some idea of what to do or say. The only thing he knew was that he must not let go before Mitch did.

It was a long ten minutes later when, hiccuping and gasping for air, Mitch released his grip. He wiped his eyes and his nose with one sleeve and flopped back in his chair.

Trying to ignore the aching and trembling of his own arms, Runt steadied himself on the chair. He cautiously eased himself from his bruised knees onto the balls of his feet. He took a deep breath and held it while he examined his friend. The redness was fading from Mitch's cheeks and his breathing had slowed, but he looked so far beyond exhausted that Runt couldn't think of a word that would describe it.

Just when Runt had decided that Mitch had, indeed, fallen asleep, he opened his eyes. A crow cawed loudly and they both tracked its flight to the top of a pine tree. Mitch glanced at Runt and inched himself higher in his chair. "Thanks."

"Sure." Runt forced his knees to unbend, wincing as pain radiated up and down his legs. When at last he felt steady on his feet, he looked at Mitch again. "You OK?"

"Yeah." He tipped his head to the right. "C'mon. I want to show you something. And I *will* answer your question. I just need to recover a little first."

Runt's mind scrambled to remember what question he might have asked but came up blank. Feeling dizzy and in need of recovery time himself, he trailed after the chair.

The afternoon breeze had grown stronger and Runt became aware that the left shoulder of his shirt was damp. By the time they stopped again, it was dry.

"Have a seat." Mitch indicated the grass in front of him. Greens flickered in brightness and shadow as the breeze stirred the branches of the willow behind him.

Runt sat down slowly. He was only beginning to come out of shock. He couldn't remember the last time he'd hugged, or been hugged by, anyone. And he *knew* he had never in his life shared an embrace of that intensity. He hoped that there wouldn't be another one on this afternoon's agenda. If Mitch held out his arms again, Runt wasn't sure he'd be able to keep himself from running in the opposite direction.

"Pretty, isn't it?" Mitch surveyed their surroundings with proprietary approval.

They were at the top of a small rise. Although the entire cemetery was neatly kept, the grass and bushes in this spot had been meticulously groomed. And the location's crowning glory was the willow tree: it was far from the largest one in the area, but its branches had been trimmed with an artist's eye, in such a way that it looked as though Mother Nature alone had been at work.

"It's beautiful."

Mitch squinted at Runt, as though assessing his sincerity, and then nodded. "It always is," he said proudly. "No matter what season. No matter what the weather is doing."

Runt wondered how, in all his cemetery wandering, he had missed this spot. "You come here a lot?"

"Depends on what you mean by a lot." Mitch settled back in his chair. "Two years ago, when it looked like I might not make it through the summer, my parents and I decided we'd better make some plans." A weak grin appeared. "You're sitting where my headstone will be."

Sputtering, his heart pounding wildly, Runt scrambled to his feet and across the grass to a spot behind the wheelchair. Only then did he realize that Mitch was doubled over in laughter.

"That was *sick!*" Runt hollered. "Not funny, Mitch!"

"It wasn't sick, it was true." Mitch chuckled again. "And the expression on your face was *exceedingly* funny!"

Runt glared at the spot where he'd been sitting. His temples were pounding and he felt sick to his stomach. How could someone who was supposed to be his friend have done that?

"Believe it or not, Robert . . ." Mitch's voice sounded strained. "I was actually trying to make this easier on you."

Runt whirled around, eyes blazing. "How was sitting on your . . . your . . ." He pointed an accusing finger at the ground. ". . . supposed to make things *easier?*"

Mitch spread his hands. "I thought that if you saw I was really OK with it, OK enough to *joke* about it . . ."

Runt's arm dropped to his side. A prickly wave of nausea swept over him, and was immediately followed by a numbing cold. When Runt finally spoke, he was astonished by the gruff steadiness of his voice.

"No more treatments."

"No more treatments," Mitch echoed softly. "It's time for the next adventure."

Runt closed his eyes and willed himself to continue breathing. *Inhale: You knew this was coming. Exhale: Didn't know! Didn't KNOW. Inhale: did know. Didn't want to face it. Exhale: Didn't know. Didn't, didn't! Inhale: Did. Exhale: Doesn't matter! Inhale: Mitch's life. Mitch's choice . . .*

Runt swayed. *Exhale: And your only decision is whether or not to be his friend while it happens.*

Runt opened his eyes and forced himself to look at Mitch. For the first time in a long time, he didn't see the hairless eyebrows or the pallor of Mitch's skin. Instead, he saw the quiet determination of the baseball picture.

"Your mom?" he finally asked. "Your dad?"

"They're OK," Mitch said. "Considering."

"Considering?" Runt repeated, and immediately wished he hadn't. *Considering their only child is dying, stupid!*

"Considering how much they love children, for one thing," Mitch said. "More than anything, they wanted a big family. Kids from one end of the house to the other." He squinted into the distance again. "Six months after I was born, they learned my mom had ovarian cancer. To be sure they got it all, they took out her entire reproductive system." He shrugged. "Twice, my parents started to adopt, but both times the birth mother changed her mind. They were going to try again, with two kids in foster care, but then I got sick . . ." His eyes grew bright. ". . . and they needed the money for medical bills." He swallowed hard. "That's why I'm an only child."

"I didn't know," Runt stammered, "that your mom had been sick."

"No reason you would," Mitch said matter-of-factly. "Complete remission. No recurrence. No metastasis. She's healthy as a top."

Runt smiled very briefly. "I'm glad."

"Yeah." Mitch's eyes shimmered. "She'll probably live to be ninety. And she'll never get to be a grandmother." He glanced at Runt. "*That's* the thing that bothers me most."

Runt shook his head in confusion and Mitch gave him a watery smile.

"I know it's not my fault. It's just that when Nana died, Mom told me that she'd led a good life, and that being my grandmother was one of the happiest parts of it. Ever since, I've wanted that for my mom." He looked down. "It's one of the reasons I fought so hard . . ."

Mitch's voice trailed off. There was nothing else to be said, and Runt wanted Mitch to be the one who broke the silence.

He did so, several minutes later, by demanding to know what time it was.

"Three twenty. We've got forty minutes."

"All right." Mitch backed his chair onto the asphalt path. "I've got to see Noah. You coming, or you had enough for one day?"

Runt's stomach flip-flopped. He'd had enough, all right. More than enough. But he wasn't about to abandon Mitch until he was safely back in Mrs. Curran's hands.

"Coming." He hesitated. "Does Noah know?"

"Yeah. My mom called him."

By three thirty they had reached the water fountain. Mitch gulped steadily and then looked around for signs of Noah while Runt took a turn.

"Give a shout, Robert! He'd never hear me."

Mitch pointed to where Noah was bent over a wheelbarrow full of marigolds. Runt shook his head and set off at a trot. He was NOT going to shout in a cemetery. It just wasn't respectful.

"Noah? Mitch's here."

The old man spun around. "Why didn't you say so?" he demanded and set off toward the wheelchair.

"I just *did* say so," Runt muttered. He shuffled as he retraced his steps. He wanted to give Noah and Mitch a chance to speak privately if they needed to.

"C'mon, Robert!" Mitch waved him forward. "Hurry up. We're going shopping!"

Runt shook his head. Of *course* they were going shopping. That's what cemeteries were for, wasn't it? Noah and the wheelchair rounded the back of the building closest to the gate and Runt trotted after them.

"Oh, *wow!*" Mitch was gazing at dozens of flowering bushes and grinning broadly. "These are amazing!"

"Only the best," Noah said with chin-up pride. "Hardy against the wind up there, too!"

Runt let his eyes wander over the array. He'd only seen plants this beautiful, this perfect, in magazines.

"You don't have to decide today," Noah said gruffly. "But it's got to be by the start of next week. You get first pick, but I've got three folks waiting to choose after you." He extracted a piece of paper from a plastic folder. "This'll show you how they'll go, season to season."

"Thanks, Noah." Mitch hesitated. "Sorry it took me so long to get over here."

Noah snorted. "You're not going to stop being a thorn in my side *this* far into the game, are you, boy?"

Mitch laughed. "Not a chance."

"Didn't think so," Noah growled. "Now leave me get some work done!"

Runt had been watching for the wink, and he smiled when it appeared. Noah's eyes met Runt's for a brief, confusing, and oddly tender moment, and then he departed with his customary jerking of arms and legs.

"Robert?"

Runt reluctantly shifted his gaze from Noah's retreating back to Mitch's chin. He wasn't quite ready to meet his eyes.

"You know what these are for, right?"

Runt winced. For your gravesite . . .

"Hey? I just realized how hard this might be for you."

For MEEEE?! Runt wanted to scream. *You're* the one who's dying!

"I'm sorry we haven't had more time together . . ."

For a moment, Runt wished *he* were the one dying. There was something terribly, horribly wrong about Mitch's wanting to comfort him. He shook his head and tried to refocus on Mitch's voice.

"We've gotten so close," Mitch apologized, "that I kind of forgot you weren't with me for the first go-around with hospice."

Exhaustion washed over Runt. He sank cross-legged to the ground and begged his memory to take notes. Maybe he'd be able to sort things out later.

He was aware of being watched, that Mitch was trying to gauge what he could absorb. It felt intrusive and reassuring at the same time.

"Robert?"

Why did the breeze have to smell so good? So green? So *alive?*

"What?"

"The bottom line is," Mitch's voice was lighter than it had been all day, "the situation stinks. In fact, to use an expression my parents really hate, it sucks."

Runt shifted restlessly.

"No one to blame. No targets for stones." Mitch tipped his head. "So you take control where you can."

Runt winced.

"It might seem kind of twisted for me to be excited about the bushes," Mitch admitted, "when I won't be around to enjoy them." He waited until Runt looked up. "But it helps if I can *imagine* how it will look. To know that it will be pretty for my parents."

Runt nodded.

"And for you." Mitch's eyes began to twinkle. "You'll come to visit, won't you?"

Runt stared at him for a moment, and then something bubbled up inside him that shook him to his core. It made his skin tingle and warned him that he was insane . . .

But he knew, deep down, that at this moment he was more sane than he had ever been.

He began to laugh.

And the universe righted itself when Mitch began to laugh, too.

23

"Honeybee?" Helen's brow was furrowed.

"You sick?"

Runt scowled. "I'm fine."

"You've hardly said three words in a month." She pointed to his nearly full plate. "And you ain't eating like you should."

"Just not hungry, that's all."

"Cole said he'd be late," Helen tried again. "Want to watch some TV?"

Runt shook his head. "Think I'll just get some sleep."

Helen sighed and picked up his plate. "I'll put this in the fridge, in case you want it later."

Runt crawled onto his bench. He knew that sleep was a long way off, but he didn't feel like watching anything, and he felt even less like talking.

What he really wanted, he decided, was a crystal ball. He wanted to know what to expect when he arrived at the Currans' in the morning.

Over the last few weeks there had been days when he would have sworn that Mitch was not sick at all. Days when he'd been full of energy, played practical jokes, and eaten two sandwiches at lunch. But there had also been days when he could do no more than watch a movie from his bed and had refused even juice.

Twice, after what Mrs. Curran referred to as "bad nights," Mitch had been sleeping when Runt arrived. Both times, she'd asked him to stay for lunch anyway, but he'd declined. Not because he didn't like Mrs. Curran—he *did* like her, a whole lot. But he knew she would try to get him to talk about his feelings, and he didn't want to do that.

What he felt most, when he allowed himself to feel at all, was how horribly unfair it was that Mitch was dying when Cole was perfectly healthy. But then, there hadn't been much fair about Mercy or Hope's dying, either . . .

He turned his pillow over and scrunched it tight. How he wished Ma had let them go to their funerals. At least he and Helen had had a chance to say goodbye to their graves. Mary and Eve hadn't even had that.

Runt let his mind wander back to the cemetery in Farnham, back to the family gathered around his mother's coffin. Back to the bored preacher. Back to his aunts, tight-lipped and resigned. Family duty had called, and they had answered. He wondered how Aunt Ruth was making out with Laura, and how Mary and Eve were doing with Aunt Grace. He wondered if they'd ever see each other again . . .

He should write to them, he supposed, but what would he say? "I hope you're doing all right. P.S. I made a friend, but he's dying . . ."

He snorted in despair and rolled over. Letter writing sure hadn't produced much where finding the Millers was concerned. Three envelopes had been returned marked "addressee unknown," and one had been returned with a note that said,

"We're not the people you're looking for." There had been no response to the rest.

Mitch had tried to be encouraging. "It's August, Robert. Lots of people travel and put their mail on hold."

In the middle of that conversation, a woman from hospice had arrived to help Mitch plan his funeral service. Although Mitch had urged him to stay, Runt had mumbled his good-byes and departed in haste. He understood that Mitch needed to take control of whatever he could, but he couldn't bring himself to listen to Mitch talk about what he'd begun to refer to as "the farewell party."

Aching for things to be different, he drifted into a fitful sleep.

". . . THAT'S MY MOTTO, AND I LIVE BY IT!"

Runt was instantly awake. The lights were on and Cole was standing in the middle of the kitchen, a half-empty bottle of beer in his hand. The way he was swaying and the loudness of his voice told Runt it wasn't the first beer he'd had.

"Winners take intelligent risks." He took a swig from the bottle. "Losers take stupid ones!" He cackled, a raucous sound, and Runt shuddered.

"Cole?" Helen's voice was soothing. "It's late. C'mon to bed now."

"It's a night to celebrate!" He emptied the bottle in a single gulp and took another one from the fridge. "Cel-e-BRATE, you hear?"

He laughed again and staggered toward the far end of the trailer. The door slid closed and the light went off. Runt forced his mind away from what might be happening in the other room. Mitch's face appeared, haggard and devoid of color. Mercy . . .

Hope . . . Ma . . . He could find no refuge, not even in sleep, and he awoke completely exhausted.

~

"MITCH HAD A BAD NIGHT," MRS. CURRAN ADMITTED. "BUT HE'S awake and wants to see you." She smiled. "You got another letter."

Runt gave her a quick smile in return. "I won't stay long."

Outside of Mitch's door, he took a deep breath and reminded himself that standing in the hall wasn't going to change anything. He knocked once and stepped into the room.

Mitch was lying in bed, his eyes closed. There was a bluish tinge to his skin that Runt had never noticed before.

"Hey, Mitch," he called softly.

"Hey." A weak grin appeared, but his eyes remained closed. "On the dresser."

Runt picked up an envelope addressed to Robert Remick, c/o Curran.

"C'mon." Mitch wheezed a little. "Open it."

Runt wrestled with the flap and unfolded a single sheet of paper.

> Dear Robert,
> My name is Jeanette Norwood, and Doris Miller was my mother's sister. Quinn Miller was my uncle (by marriage).

Was. They were both dead.

> I think they must have been the Millers that you visited as a child, since your description of the totem

pole so closely matches the one I remember. I'm
sorry to say that Aunt Doris passed away two years
ago. Uncle Quinn died in May, and the lodge was
sold as part of his estate . . .

"Well?" Mitch's eyes fluttered open. "Is it them?"

Runt hesitated for a fraction of a second, and then gave
Mitch the biggest smile he could muster. "It's them!"

"I *knew* it!" Mitch laughed and his eyes closed again. "I
knew it!"

In spite of himself, Runt grinned. "Thanks, Mitch. Thanks
a million."

"Welcome," Mitch whispered. "Sleep now . . ."

"ok," Runt said. "See you tomorrow."

He tiptoed from the room. Mrs. Curran was just coming up
the stairs.

"He's asleep."

"I expected he would be pretty quickly." She tipped her head.
"Was the letter from the people you'd hoped to hear from?"

Runt nodded. "Mitch found them."

Above her dark circles, Mrs. Curran's eyes twinkled brightly.
"I'm so glad, Robert, and Mitch must have been ecstatic. He
really wanted *this* letter to be the right one. He wanted to have
done something special for you."

"He sure did!" Runt forced himself to smile again. "See you
tomorrow."

~

THERE WAS ONLY ONE PLACE RUNT COULD THINK OF TO GO, only one place he could stand to be. He headed for the cemetery. He wasn't sure whether he really, really wanted to see Noah, or whether he really, really didn't.

He wandered among the footpaths, heading toward the older section without making a conscious decision to do so. Half an hour later, he came across a stone bench that seemed, somehow, an invitation to lie down. He lay back on the hard surface and covered his eyes with one arm.

Lord, he was tired. He was not-enough-sleep-tired. He was waiting-tired. He was worrying-tired. He was uncertain-tired. He was unanswered-questions-tired . . .

The full impact of Jeanette Norwood's letter began to sink in. He realized that he was also loss-of-last-hope tired, and drifted into the oblivion that had eluded him the night before.

At dusk, he awoke. The oppressive heat of the day had passed and the shadows beneath the trees had lengthened. For the first time in weeks he felt truly rested, and somehow at peace. He sat up, slowly and deliberately. There was no need to hurry. Mitch would let him know when it was time.

~

RUNT OPENED HIS EYES TO THE MISTY LIGHT OF A CLOUDY quarter-moon coming through the window of his bedroom in the old Farnham house. Before he could figure out how he'd gotten back here, he heard a light rapping on the door. He propped himself on one elbow and listened.

"Hey, kid!"

Runt smiled into the darkness.

"Don't you know you get stupid if you cut school?" A wide grin appeared on Mitch's face. "Or don't you care about getting stupid?"

Better to be stupid than a lunatic!

"Hey?"

What?

"It's Robert from here on. Robert the Bruce, not Runt, ok?"

Runt caught his breath. How had Mitch even known?

"See ya, Robert!"

He closed his eyes. *See ya, Mitch.*

24

Peppertree Drive was silent and serene. Number 563 looked the way it always did, with a single exception: parked behind the familiar maroon van was a small dark green station wagon.

He still hadn't met Mr. Curran—the invitation to dinner had been lost among Mitch's medical needs and visits from hospice—but the prospect of doing so was somehow not intimidating. Robert crossed the damp grass and sat down on the bottom porch step to wait.

"ROBERT?"

He jerked his head up. Mrs. Curran was peering down at him with worried eyes.

"How long have you been sitting there?"

Blushing, he got to his feet. "Awhile," he admitted.

"Come in." The door opened wider. "Please, come in."

They stopped, as if it had been prearranged, in the middle of the front hall. Tears welled up in Mrs. Curran's eyes. "Mitch . . ."

Robert nodded. "I know."

Mrs. Curran tipped her head to one side. "But how . . . ?"

Robert looked at the floor and shrugged very slightly. "He said good-bye. About three o'clock this morning."

"Maureen?" A deep voice floated down the stairs. "Who is it?"

Mrs. Curran blinked rapidly and found her voice. "David? It's Robert."

Soft footsteps came down the stairs. Mr. Curran was taller than his wife, but he was the same comforting, plump shape. He was wearing a green-and-blue plaid shirt, wrinkled navy blue pants, and white socks. His fair hair was thinning on top, and he, too, had dark circles under his eyes. At the bottom of the stairs, he reached forward to shake hands.

"David Curran." His hand was warm and dry, and kindness and strength shone from his brown eyes. "Very, *very* glad to meet you, Robert."

"Glad to meet you, Mr. Curran." He looked back and forth between Mitch's parents. "I just came to say . . ." He faltered.

"Robert." Mrs. Curran raised her hands and gently cupped his face. "You don't have to *say* anything." She gave him a gentle, lopsided smile. "No one could have been a better friend to Mitch than you were."

"We're both very grateful for that friendship." Mr. Curran's voice was husky. "Mitch thought the world of you."

Robert's cheeks began to burn, and he was relieved when Mrs. Curran let her hands fall. She looked toward the landing at the top of the stairs. "Would you like to have a moment alone with him?"

"No, thanks," he mumbled. "We had one. Last night."

Mr. Curran gave him a puzzled look and turned to his wife. She slowly shook her head.

"Somehow, Mitch said good-bye to Robert." She put a hand on his shoulder. "Will you have breakfast with us?"

Robert's stomach twisted. "Thanks, but I'd better get going."

Mitch's parents exchanged worried glances.

"Are you OK?" Mrs. Curran asked softly.

"Yeah." He gave them a weak smile. "I'm OK."

"All right." Mrs. Curran took a deep breath. "The service will probably be Friday. If you'll call us tonight, we'll be able to tell you what time."

"We'd like you to sit with the family," Mr. Curran added.

Robert suddenly felt as though he were suffocating. "Thank you," he managed to say.

The Currans followed him to the door. "We really appreciate your having come, Robert."

He gave them another brief smile and hurried down the steps.

~

"*IT'S ROBERT FROM HERE ON. ROBERT THE BRUCE, NOT RUNT, OK?*"

Robert shook his head. Whenever Mitch had called him Robert the Bruce, he'd known it was both a compliment and a challenge. He knew that Robert the Bruce had freed Scotland from control by the English, but nothing else about him . . .

The librarian was delighted to help. Over the course of the afternoon, Robert learned that in addition to being a great military tactician, Robert the Bruce took a personal interest in the lives of his officers and spoke several languages. He was also a compassionate man with a wonderful sense of humor. Robert left the library deep in thought. Mitch had given him a lot to live up to.

~

"WE'RE GOING TO THE *LOBSTER POT* FOR SUPPER!" HELEN WAS pink and nearly breathless with excitement. "Cole says we can order *anything* on the menu, and you can come!"

"No, thanks."

Helen's face fell. "Now Runt, don't be like that . . ."

"Robert."

"What?"

He lifted his chin. "My name is Robert."

"'Course it is . . ." Helen's eyebrows drew together.

"I don't want to be called Runt anymore," he said firmly. "And I am not going with you."

"If you don't come, it'll spoil Cole's good mood! *Please?*"

Robert folded his arms. "No."

Helen went to the far end of the trailer and slid the door closed with a loud bump. When the truck pulled up and Cole beeped the horn, she marched through the kitchen without looking at him. When the sound of the truck's engine died away, Robert sighed—a mixture of sorrow and relief. He hated being at odds with Helen, but he was extremely glad that he'd be alone for the evening.

He decided to call the Currans first. He fished in the coin jar, headed for the pay phone, and dialed.

"Hello?"

"Mrs. Curran? It's Robert."

"Hello, Robert. I'm so glad you called."

There were many voices in the background, and someone close to the telephone suddenly laughed. Robert scowled.

"The service will be at eleven on Friday. We'll be leaving here about ten fifteen. Can you be here by then, or would you like us to pick you up?"

"I can be there. Thanks."

"All right, then." There was a pause. "How are you doing?"

"OK." He hesitated. "How about you?"

"We're both pretty tired, but we've got friends and family here, and that's helping."

A wave of loneliness rose through Robert's chest and tightened his throat.

"Robert?"

"Sorry. See you on Friday."

"Ten fifteen. Good night."

He replaced the receiver and walked back to the trailer deep in thought. Mitch was the first real friend he'd ever had, so it was hard for him to imagine how having friends around might help. But he understood about family. Even though they hadn't talked about how they felt, it had been comforting to be with his sisters when Mercy and Hope and Ma had died . . .

He climbed the steps, decided he wasn't hungry, and flopped onto his bench. Helen didn't even know Mitch existed, much less that he'd died. He tried to remember if he'd made a conscious decision not to tell her about Mitch, and concluded he hadn't.

At first, there hadn't been anything to tell—he'd just been a weird-looking pest. And once he'd started going to Mitch's house on a regular basis, once they'd become friends, it had been a happy secret to keep. He'd supposed that eventually he'd tell her, but when Mitch got sicker, he hadn't wanted to talk. And now that he was dead, there wasn't anything to talk *about . . .*

Mitch's service! What was he going to wear? He stood up and looked down at his jeans—the black ones, the ones Helen had said were "dressier for going anywhere." The knees were badly faded. And he couldn't wear a T-shirt to a funeral . . .

He'd have to go shopping. He had his sixty dollars, and there was that secondhand shop near the library. He'd just have to hope they'd have some things in his size.

THE FOLLOWING AFTERNOON, SATISFIED WITH HIS PURCHASES, Robert headed back to the trailer. The woman who ran the shop had sized him up with an expert eye and soon had pulled two pairs of pants and three shirts from the overcrowded racks. Everything fit, and between them, they decided on a pair of tan pants, a yellow shirt with a button-down collar, and a brown-and-yellow striped tie. The woman convinced him that he needed a belt, that having one was worth an extra fifty cents, and he'd added one to the pile.

He secreted the clothes inside his bench, everything but the tie. He'd never owned one, and thought he'd better practice making the knot. Half an hour later, he gave up. No matter how he tried to wind the slippery cloth around itself, the result looked nothing like he knew it should.

Thursday night he considered asking Cole to show him how to knot the tie, but he and Helen were watching television together and laughing. He decided that Mitch would understand if he attended the service without one.

25

Robert examined his reflection again. He looked fine, but he'd look better with the tie. Helen was gone and Cole was still asleep, so he slipped the tie into his pocket and began tracing the familiar route to Peppertree Drive. Halfway there, it occurred to him that this would probably be the last time he'd ever make this journey.

He arrived at five minutes past ten. Mr. Curran was just opening the door of the van. He caught sight of Robert and smiled.

"Good morning, Robert!"

Mr. Curran was wearing a light gray suit—and a dark gray tie. Robert crossed the lawn and shyly took the brown-and-yellow one from his pocket.

"I'm sorry," he stammered. "I don't know how . . ."

Mr. Curran smiled again, gently this time. "Let me show you." He stepped behind Robert and deftly worked the tie under his collar. "The secret is to start with this side *really* short. Now, you wind the long end around twice, and come up through the hole . . ." He demonstrated. ". . . and then down through here . . ." He slid the knot neatly to the top button. ". . . and there you have it!"

Robert looked down and grinned. "Thanks."

The front door closed with a small bang and Mrs. Curran came down the steps. She was wearing a navy blue dress and a silver pendant, and she had a purse under one arm. Her face was pale and her eyes were red, but she, too, smiled.

"Don't *you* look handsome!" She ran one hand down his cheek and turned to her husband. "All set?"

He nodded. "I'm glad you got here a little early, Robert. Turns out we're picking someone up on the way."

"One of Mitch's teachers," Mrs. Curran explained. "She's in a chair, and this will make it easier for her."

Mr. Curran pointed to the small seat at the back of the van. "I'm afraid we'll have to ask you to wedge yourself in there."

Robert climbed in. Moments later, they pulled onto an expressway. They passed only two exits before pulling off again. Three traffic lights later they stopped in front of the tallest building Robert had ever seen. A uniformed man was waiting next to a silver-haired woman in a wheelchair.

The van door rolled open and the lift began its descent.

". . . so good of you . . ." The woman's voice was high-pitched and she spoke in gasps. ". . . when you have so many other things on your minds just now."

"Happy to do it, Mrs. G.," Mr. Curran assured her. "Let's get you on board."

Rubber squeaked against metal and the lift began to rise.

"And who is *this* young man?" The woman smiled, but Robert could tell that her bright black eyes were making a detailed inventory of his appearance.

"Someone very special, Mrs. G. This is Robert Remick, Mitch's closest friend these last few months." Mr. Curran gave him a quick wink. "Robert? Mrs. Grabowski, Mitch's kinder-garten teacher."

Mrs. Grabowski laughed, a deep throaty chuckle that con-trasted sharply with her voice. "Mitch was in the very last class I taught, and what a glorious end to my career he was!"

In spite of himself, Robert smiled.

"Never *saw* such an imp!" Mrs. Grabowski shook her head. "Bright as a penny, too. Miles ahead of his classmates."

The van door slammed and the engine restarted.

"Tell you a story, Robert," Mrs. Grabowski offered in a confi-dential manner. "Another teacher was looking after the class for a few minutes, someone the children weren't very fond of. When I got back, the entire class was laughing, and the substitute was standing next to Mitch with her mouth open." She paused to chuckle again. "She'd challenged him to read a page out loud from *The Cat in the Hat,* and he'd *done* it!"

Robert pictured the scene and grinned.

"Another time, I'd been out sick for a day. The woman who'd covered my class asked me how many red-headed children there were in my room." She shook with laughter. "She thought there were at least three, and Mitch was the only one!"

Robert was worried about how these stories were affecting the Currans, but the laughter from the front seat reassured him. Mrs. Grabowski continued to tell "Mitch tales" until they pulled into the parking lot of an enormous church made of dark gray stone.

A man in a black suit directed them to a parking place near the side door. Another black suit whisked the spot clear of orange plastic cones. It was a good thing a spot had been saved for the Currans. The parking lot was completely full, and there were two school buses and a large hospital shuttle parked along the driveway. People milled on the lawns and sidewalks and drifted in small groups toward the open doors at the front of the church.

With the help of the men in the black suits, they got Mrs. Grabowski down and into the hands of a former colleague who steered her up a ramp. The black suits then ushered the Currans and Robert to a side door. They almost seemed like bodyguards, the way they formed a protective circle around them and called, "The Currans look forward to greeting you after the service!" to anyone who attempted to attract their attention.

The vestibule was cool and very dark, and everyone paused to allow his or her eyes to adjust.

"Mo, babe . . ." A tall red-haired woman appeared from the shadows and bent down to hug Mrs. Curran. They rocked back and forth, and when they parted, both of their faces were streaming with tears.

"Pats—you made it." Mrs. Curran drew in a ragged breath. "Thank you."

"That's Maureen's oldest sister," Mr. Curran whispered to Robert. "She was in Venezuela when she got the news."

"Please, everyone, this way."

They moved into a small room with bright yellow walls. A quartet of black suits murmured requests for quiet. The room's occupants—perhaps twenty in all—settled down and Robert began to hear strains of organ music. The black suit who appeared to be the leader checked his watch, turned to Mr. Curran, and inclined his head.

"Maureen and I would like to thank you for being here." His voice wavered only slightly. "And for having been part of Mitch's life."

His eyes filled with tears and Mrs. Curran took his hand. He gave her a quick smile and then nodded to the leader.

"This way, please. Mr. and Mrs. Curran?"

Mrs. Curran started forward and Mr. Curran gently steered Robert into line behind her. Feet shuffled and voices whispered behind them. Ahead of them, the organ music grew louder. It sounded like nothing Robert had ever heard before. It was deep and haunting and made the air vibrate. It filled him with longings he could not name and an apprehension that made it difficult to breathe.

They were directed to a pew at the front of the church. Even in his numbed state, Robert was aware of rows of people standing at the sides and the back of the church and of the heat generated by the tightly packed bodies. Mrs. Curran reached the end of their pew, collected a booklet from the seat, and sat down. Robert did the same. Only after Mr. Curran had been seated did he look up.

In the center of the floor, above a white cloth with a gold border, stood a dark brown casket. It gleamed softly, reflecting the glow of candles that stood on brass standards to either side of it. Next to them were two large vases holding exquisite arrangements of white lilies. In the vase closest to them there was also a single, much smaller blossom—an orange tiger lily.

"Just the way he wanted it," Mrs. Curran whispered.

Mr. Curran reached behind Robert to give her shoulder a squeeze and she gave him a watery smile. Robert fastened his eyes on the cover of the little booklet. "A Celebration . . ."

The words began to swim. What was there to celebrate, for Pete's sake? Mitch was *dead*. He blinked hard. "A Celebration of the Life of Mitchell James Curran."

Rustling filled the church as those who were not already standing got to their feet. Numbly, Robert stood. *A celebration?*

A man approached the lectern and began to speak. His voice sounded thin, as though he were far, far away. The buzzing inside Robert's head grew louder. A celebration. *A celebration of the LIFE of . . .*

Memories began to pulse at the back of his neck. They pushed their way up and out in waves of heat. He closed his eyes against them and willed the thin voice to greater volume. His struggle was interrupted when Mrs. Curran took his hand and gently pulled him back down onto the pew. A woman in a dark purple dress began to read something. Mr. Curran opened his booklet, held it toward Robert, and pointed to "Prayer of Invocation."

Robert nodded and looked up at the woman. Her mouth was moving, but he couldn't hear her words. What he heard instead was the voice of a sheriff, the officer who had told them that Mercy had drowned . . .

They hadn't even heard that from their own mother. And they never saw her again. They hadn't been allowed to say good-bye, much less been given the chance to *celebrate* her life . . .

People were standing again, singing this time. Robert didn't even attempt to follow the words in the hymnal Mrs. Curran was holding. The memories would not be stayed. He was back home, climbing the stairs after school, looking forward to making Hope smile. Reaching down to wake her. He closed his eyes and shook his head, but shivered violently as he felt again the coolness of her skin. The room began spinning around him . . .

Panting, he forced his eyes open.

"Robert?" He was sitting again, and Mr. Curran's arm was around his shoulders. "You all right?"

Robert nodded. Little rivers of sweat ran down his back and his palms were damp. Desperate to keep his mind from wandering backward, he turned to look at the crowd. One face among the blurry hundreds caught his eye—a pretty little brown-skinned girl whose hair was braided and held in place with pink barrettes. Where had he seen her before?

Her name suddenly popped into his mind. Cindy—the little girl who had been going to radiation for the first time. She'd been frightened, and Mitch had made her smile. He'd given her something from his bag of tricks . . .

The church suddenly erupted in laughter and Robert gasped. Churches weren't places to laugh! And certainly not during a funeral. His eyes darted between the Currans. They were both smiling. He looked toward the lectern. The man who was speaking grinned, and a moment later, the church was filled with laughter again.

Robert's temples pounded as he was suddenly transported back to his mother's funeral. No laughter. No music. No celebration . . .

Around him, people were standing and reaching for hymnals again. Robert glanced up at Mitch's casket and his chest filled with a pain that radiated down his arms and knifed into his stomach. His shoulders jerked as he heaved in the overheated, salty air. He clenched his teeth, but when he looked again at the tiger lily, his eyes overflowed and he sobbed.

He would never see Mitch again.

26

The traffic light turned from green to yellow and
the car slowed.

"I can walk from here," Robert offered.

The bearded man at the wheel shook his head. "David said
right to the door, and that's where we're going."

Robert lay back against the seat. He really didn't feel up to
walking. He barely had the energy to hope that no one would
be home.

"Where do I turn?" the driver inquired several minutes later.
Robert had been introduced, but he couldn't remember the
man's name. He couldn't remember much of anything besides
crying until he could scarcely breathe, and feeling Mr. Curran's
arm around his shoulders.

"About another mile." They rode in silence until Robert spied
the Airview sign. "There. On the left."

The car bumped its way up the driveway. With relief Robert
noted that Cole's truck was gone.

"That one." He pointed and the car came to a halt. "Thank
you."

"Sure thing," the driver replied. "You'll be all right?"

Robert nodded. "Thanks again."

The car didn't move until the door to the trailer had closed behind him. When he could no longer hear it, he crawled onto his bench and closed his eyes.

HE AWAKENED IN A GLOOMY DUSK, WISHING HE HAD NOT. HIS head hurt and he was desperately thirsty.

"Runt?" Helen called softly. "You awake?"

The emptiness in his chest threatened to consume him.

"Honeybee?"

Scowling, he turned toward the wall. Helen crossed the room and sat down on the edge of his bench. "What's going on? Why are you all dressed up?"

"Because I felt like it."

"You been looking for work?"

"No."

"Then what?"

Robert sighed. It wasn't like Helen to be this persistent. "I went to a funeral, OK?"

There was a stunned silence behind him. It was broken by the loathsome purr of Cole's truck. The engine died, a door slammed, and the trailer door opened.

"Hey, Cole." Helen stood up.

Cole grunted. "What's the matter with him?"

"Leave him be," Helen said sharply. In a much softer voice she added, "I'll fix you some supper."

Cole grunted again. "Put on something decent. We're going out."

Twenty minutes later Helen leaned over and whispered, "Try and eat something, all right? And there's a cherry soda in the cupboard."

"Thanks," he whispered back.

Robert stayed where he was until his thirst forced him to his feet. The kitchen light hurt his swollen eyes and he turned it off. The soft gleam through the windows was enough to make shadows of the cupboards. He found the soda, filled a glass with ice, and carried both things to the table. The sweet odor of artificial cherry wafted toward him and his memory flew back to his arrival in Westfield. He snorted softly. That was a lifetime ago. That had been before Mitch.

He poured the soda deliberately, listening to the ice crack, and then drained the glass in six satisfying gulps. He refilled the glass and emptied it again, slowly this time. The cold sweetness was a barrier to thoughts about Mitch and a future in Westfield without him.

~

THE DAYS THAT FOLLOWED WERE A BLUR OF EXHAUSTION AND sleeplessness, and listless walks to the top of the hill he'd fallen down that first day. His promise to visit the Currans—a promise they'd extracted the morning of the funeral—haunted his conscience, but he couldn't bring himself to go. Nor could he bring himself to visit the cemetery. He could only look at it from the top of the hill.

He ate, mechanically and without tasting the food, whenever Helen cooked and insisted. The evening after the funeral, she'd tried to get him to talk.

"This funeral you went to," she asked tentatively. "Who was it for?"

Robert poked at his beans. How was he supposed to describe Mitch? How could he begin to explain who he'd been?

"This kid I met."

"How old was he?"

"Thirteen."

"How did he die?"

"He had cancer."

Helen winced. "Where'd you meet him?"

"In the cemetery."

They ate in silence for several minutes before Helen said, "That where you've been spending your days? With this friend?"

Robert nodded.

"You must be hurting," she said softly and let the matter drop.

~

ON A LATE AUGUST NIGHT, ROBERT LAY AWAKE IN THE DARKNESS. Cole had come home at two thirty, drunk and in high spirits, and it had taken Helen the better part of an hour to quiet him down. Since then, Robert had tried, unsuccessfully, to will himself back to sleep. The clock on the stove now read 3:52.

The humidity was low and the night sounds that came through Robert's window seemed amplified. Gravel began to crunch, and it sounded vaguely like the crackling of a fire. Two cars arrived within seconds of each other and stopped very close to the trailer. A deep voice murmured and was answered by a higher murmur. Robert was trying to choose between the warmth of his blanket and satisfying his curiosity when he was jolted upright by a tremendous banging on the trailer door.

"Open up!" *Thump. Thump. Thump.* "Police! Open up!"

27

The banging continued. "Open up! This is the police!"

Robert held himself completely still. Lights were coming on in trailers all around them. The door to the far end slid open and the kitchen light went on. Cole was wearing a wrinkled white T-shirt and he was hauling a pair of jeans up over his boxers as he walked. Another car came to a halt nearby. The slamming of a door was followed by barking.

"Hang on, hang on!" Cole muttered. He yanked open the door and snapped, "It's the middle of the night, for God's sake!"

"Please step back, sir."

"What's this all about?" Cole demanded.

"Please step back, sir."

Cole did so, and four police officers, three men and a woman, crowded into the tiny kitchen.

"Are you Cole Martin?" the shortest officer asked.

"Maybe, maybe not." He folded his arms. "Why?"

Helen appeared behind Cole. Her arms were crossed over her chest, and she was holding one hand to her mouth.

"Sir," the female officer said, "Unless you want to add resisting arrest to the charges, you'd better answer his question."

Cole looked back to the shortest officer. "Yeah, I'm Cole Martin. Now what's this all about?"

"We have warrants for your arrest and to search your vehicle."

The tallest of the officers took a pair of handcuffs from his belt and stepped behind Cole. Robert heard a small click. Cole's jaw was set and his eyes were mere slits, but he didn't struggle.

"Possession and sale of methamphetamine." The shortest officer read from a paper. "Four Class 6 felonies, including one sale to a minor." The officer gave Cole an icy smile. "That redhead at the gas station in Dunkirk? That was my niece, and she's all of seventeen."

The tallest officer began to pat the legs of Cole's jeans.

"You have the right to remain silent," the female officer began. "Anything you say can be used against you in a court of law. You have the right to consult an attorney . . ."

Robert's eyes darted around the room. Helen looked as though she might be sick at any moment. The fourth officer was holding a pad of paper in one hand and a pen in the other. "Your name, ma'am?"

Helen's mouth opened and closed several times. "Helen," she finally croaked. "Helen Remick."

The officer glanced at Cole. "You married?"

Helen shook her head.

"Will you get him some shoes?"

Helen blinked rapidly and retreated. She returned with a pair of black loafers, placed them on the floor next to Cole, and stepped back without looking at him. He maneuvered them onto his feet, and the tallest officer guided him toward the door. He spoke not a word, and he didn't look back.

The female officer tipped her head toward Helen and the shortest officer nodded. "Bring her in for questioning." He headed for the door. "Get her dressed and then call Larry in."

Helen and the female officer disappeared and the remaining officer glanced around the room. "And what have we here?" He smiled. "Who are you?"

"Robert," he stammered. "Helen's brother."

"No relation to Cole Martin, then?"

Robert shook his head.

"Know anything about his dealing drugs?"

"No!" Robert yelped. "He never said *anything* about what he does!" His heart was pounding so hard that his ears hurt. "His phone rings and he just takes off!"

The officer nodded. "He plays things close to the chest," he conceded. "Took us awhile to get onto him."

The two women came back into the kitchen.

"We've got the meth sales on video," the officer continued, "but it's routine to search premises for other contraband."

The female officer walked to the door and held it open. "Larry? All yours."

Toenails scraped against wood and a German shepherd scrambled into the room with a round-faced officer at the other end of his leash. "Hunt, Carson! Hunt!"

The dog's tail wagged furiously and he began sniffing the bottoms of the kitchen cupboards. He then put his paws on the counter and sniffed the air near the upper ones. He moved around the edge of the room, nose twitching, at an incredibly rapid pace.

"Would you mind getting up, son?"

Robert scurried across the room and stood next to the sink. The benches were opened and the dog peered inside. He found nothing of interest, and the team moved on to the bathroom. Robert heard the shower door open and close, and the lid being lifted from the back of the toilet. Seconds later, they moved to the front of the trailer. Robert glanced at his sister. Helen looked back at him with stricken eyes and shook her head: she'd had no idea that Cole was dealing drugs.

"Nothing doing inside," Carson's human partner announced cheerfully. "But I'm taking side bets on the truck."

The three officers went down the steps and the Remicks followed. There were people in nightclothes in front of trailers up and down the lane. Carson sniffed the right rear tire of Cole's truck and immediately began to bark and whine.

"Bingo!" Larry grinned and rubbed Carson's head. "Good boy," he crooned.

"I'll get a boot." The officer who had spoken to Robert opened the trunk of his squad car, removed a rusty yellow contraption, and carried it to the far side of the truck. Still shaking, Robert stepped forward to watch.

The officer bent down, fitted the boot around the left front tire, and locked it. It was now impossible to drive the truck.

"Do you have some I.D. with you, ma'am?"

Helen nodded. "How long will this take?"

"Shouldn't be more than a couple of hours," the female officer assured her. Then she lifted her chin toward Robert. "Is he all right to stay on his own?"

Helen nodded and whispered, "Be back as soon as I can."

With a combination of disbelief and terror, Robert watched

her get into the squad car. Helen tried to give him a smile, but her eyes were so full of fear that her attempt backfired.

Within sixty seconds the road was empty of cars and, except for one group of rubberneckers, empty of people as well. Robert climbed the steps to the trailer and quietly closed the door. The clock on the microwave said 4:18. Less than half an hour since the police had begun banging.

A wave of dizziness washed over him and he steadied himself against the counter. Cole was a drug dealer. He'd been arrested and taken away in handcuffs, and Helen had been taken in for questioning. He was alone in Cole's trailer. In Cole's drug deal-ing trailer, with Cole's drug dealing truck parked outside. And who knew when Helen would be back?

What if she didn't *come* back?

Helen's horrified expression had made *him* certain she hadn't known anything about Cole's drug dealing, but the police didn't know her the way he did. What if they didn't believe her? What if they arrested her, too?

The image of Helen locked in a jail cell tipped him over the edge, and his body demanded action. Thirty seconds later, he was dressed. He scribbled a note, pulled on his sneakers, and set off toward the only potential source of help left in his world.

28

He ran from the moment his feet touched the
ground until he reached the Currans' front lawn. He could
barely breathe, but panic pushed him forward. The Currans
were surely asleep. He didn't want to wake them, but where
else could he turn?

He climbed the steps and rapped on the door with his
knuckles. He stood still, chest heaving, praying for someone to
open it. Long, still minutes passed. Please! He knocked again,
harder this time. *Please!*

A bird sang a lone predawn note. He glanced over his shoulder
at a sky that was still nearly black.

You are alone. The darkness mocked him. *No one cares. No
one will help.*

Noooooo!

Robert lunged for the brass knocker. He grasped it tightly
and banged it three times. The sound rattled through his body
and echoed into the air, and his legs simply folded under him.
He never heard the door open.

"Robert?" Mr. Curran gently lifted him to his feet. "What in
heaven's name is wrong?"

"My sister . . ." He choked. "They took her!"

Mr. Curran took Robert's face in both hands. "Who took her?"

"The police!"

Robert sobbed and Mr. Curran's big, solid arms drew him into a hug. "First things first," he said firmly. "A sweatshirt and something hot to drink. And when you've stopped shivering, you'll tell us the *whole* story, and we'll do whatever we can to help."

In no time at all, Robert had his hands around a cup of hot chocolate and Mr. and Mrs. Curran were pouring themselves mugs of fresh coffee.

"Now," Mr. Curran said quietly, "start at the beginning. When did the police come, and why did they take your sister?"

"About four o'clock." Robert stammered. "And there were five of them, and a dog, and they arrested Cole . . ." His words tumbled over each other. "And then they said she had to go with them!"

Mr. Curran held up one hand. "Slow down. Who is Cole?"

In bits and pieces, and in response to dozens of gentle questions from the Currans, the whole story came out. Mercy's death and Hope's death, and Helen's reason for leaving home. Not hearing from her for six years. Ma's dying and his aunts being unwilling to take on a boy. Helen's moving in with Cole to provide a home for her brother. The reason he'd missed his visit to Mitch. The letter explaining that the Millers had died. And, finally, Cole's having been charged with possession and sale of methamphetamine.

"I'm *positive* she didn't know anything about it," Robert said. "But what if they don't believe her?"

"What's your sister's given name?"

"Helen. Helen Louise Remick."

Mr. Curran gave Robert's shoulder a squeeze and stood up. "Let me make a couple of phone calls and see what I can find out."

He left the kitchen and Mrs. Curran shook her head. "What you've been through, Robert . . ."

"I'm sorry I woke you up," he stammered. "But I didn't know what else to do."

"You did exactly the right thing," Mrs. Curran said firmly. She nodded toward the window. "Sun's coming up. How about some breakfast?"

Robert had never tasted scrambled eggs as good as the ones Mrs. Curran served him. Or better toast. He swallowed his last bite as the telephone rang. A few minutes later, Mr. Curran came back into the kitchen. He was smiling.

"I have a friend who's a desk sergeant," he explained. "Your sister has been released, and no charges have been filed against her."

"Thank you." A tidal wave of relief washed through Robert and he was suddenly very sleepy.

"Will she know where you've gone?"

Robert nodded. "I left a note."

The telephone rang again and Mr. Curran went to answer it.

"I'd better get going." Robert pushed himself away from the table. "Thanks a whole lot, Mrs. Curran. For everything."

Mrs. Curran opened her mouth to protest, but before she could speak, Mr. Curran returned.

"That was your sister, Robert. Grateful to know that you're safe, but insisting that she had to go to work."

"Go to work?" Mrs. Curran sputtered. "After the *night* she's just had?"

Robert shrugged. "That's just how she is."

Mr. Curran folded his arms. "I did, however, manage to persuade her to come here for dinner." He raised one eyebrow. "Seems as though you've forgotten something . . ."

Robert gave him a blank look.

"You're thirteen today!" Mr. Curran grinned. "Happy birthday, Robert!"

Robert's eyes grew wide. It *was* the twenty-sixth! He was a teenager now . . .

"Oh, happy birthday indeed!" Mrs. Curran beamed at him. "Now, what kind of cake shall we have?" Her eyes twinkled. "How does lemon with chocolate frosting sound?"

Robert smiled. "It sounds great."

Mr. Curran looked at the clock. "I'll leave you two to work out the rest of the menu. I'd better shower and get to work myself."

Mrs. Curran turned to Robert. "The dinner menu will keep. What *you* need is some sleep!"

Robert gratefully accepted a pillow and a blanket and sank onto the living room sofa. The cushions were plump and deep and so unlike the thin padding on his bench that he fought to stay awake just to experience lying on them. He wriggled, stretched his legs, sighed happily, and drifted off.

He awoke midafternoon to find a note from Mrs. Curran: lunch was on the kitchen table, and she'd be back from the grocery store by three thirty. He ate his sandwich slowly, a kaleidoscope of images churning through his mind: Cole being handcuffed; Helen's expression as the police car pulled away; the fact that Mitch was no longer upstairs . . .

The van pulled into the driveway and he hurried to help carry in the groceries. Mrs. Curran had decided they would have spaghetti and salad and fresh Italian bread.

"I cheat a little on the sauce," she confided. "Store-bought, but with a few extras thrown in."

Robert was happy to dice tomatoes and chop parsley, glad to have something to occupy his hands and at least part of his mind. The difference between where he was now and where he'd been twelve hours ago was more than he could sort out.

At quarter to five, there was a tentative knock on the front door. Mrs. Curran gave Robert a quick smile and hurried from the room.

"You must be Helen," he heard her say. "I'm Maureen Curran, and we're so glad you could come." The door closed. "The birthday boy is in the kitchen, just in through there."

A moment later, Helen appeared in the doorway. "Hey, Runt," she said softly.

Robert stared. Helen's hair was limp and stringy and her face was nearly without color. Her uniform was wrinkled and hung far more loosely on her slender frame than he remembered. The circles under her eyes had a greenish cast to them, and it was obvious that she was struggling to keep her eyes open.

"Hey," he finally said back. "How you doing?"

Her head bobbed once. "All right." She crossed the room and handed him a package wrapped in blue-and-yellow paper. "Happy birthday."

"Thanks." Robert reached for the bow.

"None of that, now!" Mrs. Curran scolded with a smile. "Presents come *after* cake."

She scooped the box from his hands and set it on top of the refrigerator—next to two other brightly wrapped boxes Robert hadn't noticed before. His eyes grew wide, and Mrs. Curran laughed.

"You have to earn them," she said. "Keep chopping!"

Robert grinned and went back to work.

"And *you . . .*" Mrs. Curran turned to Helen. "Need some pampering. A nice long bubble bath, some herbal tea, and a nap. How does that sound?"

Robert held his breath. Helen hesitated, but finally smiled. "Sounds real nice."

29

"Smells good in here!" Mr. Curran kissed his wife and smiled at Robert.

"I'd like to let Helen sleep a little while longer," Mrs. Curran said. "Why don't you show Robert the workshop?"

Mr. Curran's whole face lit up and Robert suddenly saw his resemblance to Mitch.

"You like working with wood?"

The animation in his voice made Robert smile. "I used to make simple stuff for my sisters."

"Careful," Mrs. Curran cautioned. "You are about to enter the twilight zone of woodworking!"

"There is nothing supernatural about my workshop!" Mr. Curran thrust out his chin. "I am merely enthusiastic." He winked at Robert. "Just let me get changed and I'll give you the tour."

Mr. Curran bounded up the front stairs and Mrs. Curran rolled her eyes. "I promise to rescue you from his clutches before you die of starvation."

Three minutes later, Mr. Curran led Robert around the side of the house and into another world. The left-hand side of the garage was occupied by the van; the right side was entirely devoted to woodworking.

The workbench itself was about half the size of Cole's trailer. Robert recognized most of the tools hanging above it—hammers, saws, several types of screwdrivers—but there were others he'd never seen before.

Shelves were filled with neatly labeled boxes. A dozen glass jars were suspended from the underside of the lowest shelf. They contained nails, screws, and washers of various sizes.

Mr. Curran reached forward. "The lids are screwed into the board." He twisted a jar and it came free. "Everything's within easy reach, and the jars don't get broken."

"And you can see what's inside!"

"Right." Mr. Curran replaced the jar. "These are handy for odd jobs, but when I'm working on something special, I like to use only pegs."

He stepped to the end of the bench and opened a drawer. Inside were a dozen compartments containing wooden pegs of varying lengths and diameters.

"You use those instead of nails?"

Mr. Curran nodded. "You drill holes in the two pieces you want to join, and put the peg between them." He slid the drawer closed. "If you do it properly, the joint is much stronger than a nail or a screw. It lasts longer, it looks better, and for things you hope will last more than one generation, it just somehow seems *right* to use wood on wood."

Robert slowly nodded.

"Here." Mr. Curran stepped to the back of the garage and returned with a high chair. "See?" He pointed to several places where the wood had been pegged. Then he set the chair on the floor and tried to rock it, first from side to side, and then back and forth. It didn't budge.

"Solid as the day I finished it." He grinned. "And believe me, it got a workout!"

"Was it Mitch's?"

"It was." Mr. Curran looked down at the chair and his eyes grew bright. "The whole time I was working on it, I was hoping he'd be able to use it for his children, and they'd use it for *their* children . . ." He shook his head and carried the chair back to its place. When he returned, he continued his enthusiastic tutorial, and Robert continued to lap up every word. When Mrs. Curran called them to dinner, Robert was astonished to find they'd been in the workshop for nearly two hours.

"Hope you boys don't mind the delay." Mrs. Curran greeted them with one of Mitch's smiles. "But Helen and I have been getting to know each other and we lost track of time."

"Off with your head!" Mr. Curran declared.

Robert grinned and looked at his sister. Helen was smiling, too, and looked a hundred times better than when she arrived.

"Birthday boy first." Mrs. Curran filled a plate with spaghetti, added two ladles full of thick sauce, and handed it to Robert. "Dig right in," she urged. "Eat while it's hot!"

Robert carried his plate to the table and sat down, but he was in no hurry to begin. Since the moment he had awakened in the soft comfort of the Currans' sofa, he'd felt as though he was inside a happy dream. If the pungent aroma of the sauce was a dream, if the bright white-and-yellow kitchen was a dream, if the friendly voices around him were a dream, he wanted it all to last as long as possible.

After the others had all begun to eat and he hadn't awakened to find himself back in the trailer, Robert took his first bite.

"Mmmmm!" Mr. Curran said. "Outstanding sauce tonight, Maureen."

Mrs. Curran smiled at Robert. "I had outstanding help!"

After several attempts to draw the Remicks into conversation, the Currans had to give up. Instead, Mrs. Curran told a story about a friend of hers who'd just returned from Japan, a country the Currans hoped to visit one day. Robert and Helen both ate second helpings while they listened.

"Fun to dream about, anyway." Mrs. Curran began clearing the table. "But we won't be buying airplane tickets any time soon."

"Next traveling *we'll* be doing," said Mr. Curran, "is by moving van."

Robert looked at him in dismay. "You're moving?"

"Not right away," Mrs. Curran assured him. "It'll be at least a month until David can wind things up at the office and we can get the house packed." She gave him a sympathetic look. "There hasn't been a chance to tell you before now, Robert. We started thinking about all of this two summers ago, but we only made the final decision on Monday."

"As much as we love this house," Mr. Curran said quietly, "and the time we've spent in it . . ." He shook his head. "With Mitch gone, it would simply be too hard to stay."

"David's company has a branch office in Seneca." Mrs. Curran said brightly. "It's only twenty miles from here, so we can visit the cemetery as often as we want to. And we've found a nice house."

"It's actually outside the town—setting's almost rural." Mr. Curran added. "It even has a pond out back. Spring-fed and ice-cold!"

Robert's throat was suddenly full.

"Sounds nice," Helen said.

"Yeah," Robert finally managed. "Sounds great."

Mrs. Curran gave him a sad smile. "Didn't mean to put a damper on the evening with that news."

Robert shook his head. "No. I'm happy you found a place that you like." He forced himself to return the smile. "Honest!"

30

Robert barely heard the singing around him.
He had to be prompted to make a wish and blow out his
candles, and then he couldn't think of anything to wish for.
Everyone was looking at him and waiting. He finally sent an
unspecified prayer skyward and blew. All the candles went out,
and everyone clapped.

The cake was as delicious as the rest of the meal, but Robert
barely tasted it. He was here in Mitch's house, where Mitch *wasn't*
and where Mitch's parents, two of the kindest people he'd ever
known, soon wouldn't be . . .

"Now you can open your presents." Mrs. Curran removed
his dessert plate and set Helen's package, along with two smaller
packages, in front of him.

"Thank you."

He removed the paper from the package Helen had handed
him earlier, took off the lid, and lifted a new teal blue windbreaker from the box. It had a zip-in lining, and a hood, and
three pockets that fastened with snaps. Robert guessed that it
had cost Helen a week's pay.

"Happy birthday," she said softly.

He stared at her for a moment, looked back to the windbreaker, and stammered, "Thanks, Helen. It's great!"

"Well, your old one was getting pretty short in the sleeves . . ."

"It's a *beautiful* jacket!" Mrs. Curran exclaimed. "Practical, and as handsome as can be!"

Robert nodded. It was the nicest piece of clothing he'd ever owned.

"This one's something to wear, too." Mrs. Curran handed him a brightly wrapped package that weighed very little. Robert unwrapped it and shook loose a royal blue T-shirt. Across the front, in white letters, was printed: "CHAOS, PANIC, PANDE— MONIUM . . . my work here is done."

"It was Mitch's," Mrs. Curran explained. "He only wore it once, and I think he'd be glad for you to have it."

Robert turned the shirt around so Helen could read it.

"Thanks, Mrs. Curran."

Mr. Curran gave Helen a quick smile. "I don't know how much Robert has told you about Mitch, but that T-shirt pretty much says it all."

Helen smiled back. "Sounds like he had a lot of spirit."

"That he did!"

"One more," Mrs. Curran said brightly. "One of Mitch's favorite books, but your own brand-new copy."

Robert slowly tore away the paper from a slender black book with gold lettering on the spine. *The Prophet,* by Kahlil Gibran.

"It's not like reading a novel," Mrs. Curran explained. "It's the sort of book you dip into now and then, or turn to when you're thinking hard about a particular question."

"Thank you," he stammered.

"I hope it's been a good birthday, Robert," Mrs. Curran said quietly. "But it's also been a long day for all of us, and I think it's time we got to bed." She turned to Helen. "Guest room's only got one bed. Would you like to sleep there, or in the living room with Robert?"

Helen glanced at her brother. "I was figuring we'd go back to the trailer tonight."

"Time enough for that tomorrow, but I imagine the two of you might like to talk. Why don't I bring down a pillow and some blankets, and we'll set you up on the recliner."

Ten minutes later, Robert was settled on the sofa, Helen was curled up on the recliner, and the Currans had retired to the second floor. Robert switched off the lamp and watched his sister pull her blanket up around her shoulders.

"They're real nice people, Runt," she whispered.

"Yeah. They are."

The silence around them deepened.

"Helen?"

"Hmmm?"

"Is Cole still in jail?"

"Must be," she said sadly. "Bail was ten thousand dollars, and I don't know anybody who'd lend him that kind of money."

The silence returned.

"What we gonna do, then?" Robert finally asked. "Where we gonna live?"

"We'll figure out something." Helen's voice lacked conviction. "Go on to sleep now."

Robert awoke in early morning darkness to the smell of coffee and the sound of someone cracking eggs. He glanced at the recliner; Helen was still asleep. Silently he made his way to the kitchen. Mr. Curran, already showered and dressed, was at the stove.

"Morning! Sleep well?"

Robert nodded.

"Good. I'm just starting some pancakes. Maureen and I were up kind of late, and she's still asleep."

"So's Helen," Robert admitted. "Can I help?"

"How about setting the table?"

As the last of the pancake batter was poured onto the griddle, Mrs. Curran and Helen appeared. Mr. Curran filled four plates, set syrup on the table, and sat down.

"Maureen and I spent a long time talking last night, and we have a proposition for you."

The Remicks exchanged puzzled looks.

"Seems as though you two need a new place to live . . ."

"And the house in Seneca has three bedrooms," Mrs. Curran jumped in. "The two of us would pretty much rattle around in it by ourselves."

Robert's eyes grew wide. Was it possible? Were the Currans actually inviting them . . . ?

"A new town would also mean a fresh start," Mr. Curran added.

Helen set down her fork. "That's kind of you. But we don't take charity."

"We're not offering charity," Mr. Curran countered. "You'd work. Chip in on food, pay some rent, if that's the way you'd like to handle it."

"But we could share the house, and meals," Mrs. Curran said eagerly. "Be family to each other at holidays!"

Robert looked at Helen with pleading eyes.

"There'd be one condition, though." Mr. Curran's expression became serious. "School. For *both* of you."

Helen's mouth dropped open. "I can't go back to school!" she sputtered. "I'm nineteen years old!"

"Adult education," Mr. Curran said matter-of-factly. "Work during the day, get your high school diploma at night. Then decide whether you want a program at a junior college, or a four-year school."

College! Robert's brain bounced. Remicks didn't go to college—Aunt Ruth was the only member of the family who'd even finished high school!

"Thank you," Helen said stiffly. Blotchy red spots had appeared on her cheeks. "But we'll manage."

"Don't decide now," Mrs. Curran pleaded. "We know it's a lot to think about."

"We hope you'll at least talk it over." Mr. Curran checked his watch and got up from the table. "I've got an early meeting and I'd better get going." He kissed Mrs. Curran's cheek and departed.

Mrs. Curran turned to Helen. "Your uniform is on the bed in the guest room."

Helen hurried up the stairs, her cheeks still flushed.

Robert shoveled pancakes into his mouth, his heart beating fast.

Helen reappeared in the doorway. "Thank you . . ." She lifted one edge of her freshly ironed skirt.

"No problem," Mrs. Curran assured her. "Would you like a ride to work?"

"No, thanks." She turned to Robert. "See you later. At home." She stole a quick glance at Mrs. Curran. "Thanks again for all your kindness."

She hurried from the room, the front door opened and closed, and Mrs. Curran's shoulders fell.

"We should have waited until she got to know us a little . . ."

"Did you really mean it?" Robert couldn't contain himself any longer. "You'd really take us with you?"

Mrs. Curran nodded.

"But why?" he stammered. "Why would you take in a couple of strangers?"

Mrs. Curran gave him a sad smile. "You're hardly a stranger, Robert."

"But Helen is. You only just met her!"

"We know she's the kind of person who wanted to make a home for her brother. And who managed, against some pretty tall odds, to do it." Mrs. Curran shook her head. "David and I don't need to know much more than that."

31

At three forty-five, Robert positioned himself two doors from Hayden's Family Restaurant and set his bag of birthday presents on the pavement beside him. At five minutes after four, Helen came down the steps and walked past him without stopping.

"We're not going."

Robert snatched up the bag and trotted after her.

"We'll manage on our own, same as we have been."

"Where we gonna live, then?"

"I got tomorrow off," she retorted. "I'll find something."

"You said the boardinghouse wouldn't let us share a room!"

"We'll find something else, then."

Robert tried a different tack. "If we go with the Currans, I'll go to school!"

"*You* belong in school," she said flatly. "I don't!"

"Why not?" Robert demanded. "You're smart. Finish school, you could get a *good* job . . ."

Helen wheeled around and jabbed a finger at him. "No shame in waiting tables, Runt! It's done all right to put food in *your* belly!"

"I didn't mean it like that!"

Helen snorted and resumed her furious pace. Robert jogged until he caught up with her again. "I just meant a job where you wouldn't have to be on your feet all day."

Helen didn't respond and he tried again. "There's nothing to keep us in Westfield."

"There's nothing to take us to Seneca, either!"

"Nothing but somewhere to live! And having *friends!*"

Helen turned to glare at him. "And just what do you suppose people like them want with the likes of us?"

"What do you mean?" Robert stammered. "What's wrong with us?"

"There's *nothing* wrong with us." Helen's eyes glittered dangerously. "We don't take, we don't owe. But you've seen how they live, heard them talking college." She shook her head. "That ain't us."

Something exploded inside of Robert. "Why *couldn't* it be?"

"Time you grew up, Runt. Fairy tales don't happen in real life." Helen's voice became hard. "Fairy tales don't happen to Remicks."

"They might!" Robert's voice rose. "Maybe they could, if you'd meet them halfway!"

Helen folded her arms and looked at him through narrowed eyes. "What do you even *know* about these people?"

"I know they loved Mitch." Robert's voice shook. "And I know they helped me when I needed it."

"That's not the same as offering us a home."

"Now that Mitch's gone, they must be *lonely.*"

Helen squinted into the distance. "I've been on my own too long, Runt. I can't go back to living under someone else's roof."

"You lived under *Cole's* roof!"

"That was different."

"Yeah, if we lived with the Currans, you might miss being hit, and ordered around, and having drugs sold behind your back!"

Helen's eyes filled with tears. "I did the best I could, Runt."

"I know that!" He swallowed hard. "But you deserve better, and here's a *chance,* and you're saying no!"

Helen abruptly resumed walking. She stopped long enough to deposit two coins in a vending machine and collect a newspaper, but she didn't look back. With heavy steps and a heavier heart, Robert followed her up the road to the trailer. Cole's truck was no longer parked beside it.

By the time he climbed the steps, Helen was taking a cup of coffee from the microwave. She carried the cup and the newspaper to the far end of the trailer. From the kitchen, Robert watched her take a pen from her pocket and sit down on the floor. She opened the paper and leaned forward to peer at the tiny print.

Robert sighed hopelessly and retreated to his bench. He admired his new jacket again and smiled as he reread Mitch's T-shirt. Then he picked up *The Prophet,* opened it at random, and found himself reading a passage titled "On Friendship."

As he read he realized that Mitch had answered needs Robert hadn't even known he had. The need for connection and honesty. The need to talk about feelings that Remicks never talked about. And the need for playfulness and laughter. Robert's chest grew warm. He couldn't imagine that anyone, ever, had been more alive than Mitch . . .

He allowed the book to close. When his stomach growled, he got to his feet.

The newspaper remained spread on the floor. Helen was curled up under a blanket at one end of the sofa, apparently asleep. He tiptoed forward and knelt down to look at the ads. Only two had been circled: both one-bedroom apartments, and both more money per month than Helen made. He looked at her tear-stained cheeks and sighed. Helen could use a friend. A *real* friend, someone like Mitch, not a jerk like Cole . . .

He retreated to the kitchen. No matter where they ended up living, they'd still need to eat supper.

He had drained the macaroni and was melting margarine for the cheese sauce when he heard gravel crunching and froze.

Cole?

No—this engine had a much deeper rumble.

The police?

Holding his breath, he peeked out the window. A dark green station wagon had rolled to a stop, and Mr. and Mrs. Curran were climbing from the front seat.

32

Robert pushed open the door. "Hi."

"Hi, Robert." Mrs. Curran smiled nervously. "Hope you don't mind our just coming like this, but with your having no phone, we didn't know how else to reach you."

"How did you know where we live?"

"Hans Schumacher," Mr. Curran said. "The man who drove you home from the funeral."

"We'd really like to talk with you for a few minutes." Mrs. Curran hesitated. "Would your sister mind if we came in?"

"She won't mind. She's asleep."

He stepped back and the Currans came up the steps. "Please . . ." He pointed to the chairs at the table. "Would you like something to drink?" He turned off the stove and opened the refrigerator. "There's iced tea. And orange juice."

"Nothing for me, thanks," Mr. Curran said.

"We've just finished supper," Mrs. Curran explained. "So nothing for me, either. But thank you."

Robert closed the refrigerator door. Although he'd last seen Mr. Curran this morning, and Mrs. Curran only hours ago, it felt as though at least a month had passed, and he had no idea what to say.

"We'd like to start by apologizing," Mrs. Curran said.

Robert's mouth dropped open. Apologize? For having helped him? For having made a fuss over his birthday? For having invited them to move to Seneca?

His stomach lurched. Or were they going to apologize for having changed their minds?

"Our offer to share our home was sincere," Mr. Curran said quickly, "and it stands. But our timing could have been better. Helen had barely met us."

"So let's look at things from her point of view," Mrs. Curran said quietly. "She was forced to fend for herself from a terribly young age, and she somehow managed to do it."

"And then she took on providing for you." Mr. Curran's voice was full of admiration. "I can't *fathom* having such a responsibility at the age of nineteen."

"I know." Heat rose from Robert's neck to his ears. "But my aunts didn't want me." His voice broke. "Until after Ma died, I didn't even know if Helen was still alive!"

"Oh, Robert," Mrs. Curran whispered. "You've been through so much."

"You've *both* been through so much," Mr. Curran continued, "and you've both *lost* so much. Not only your parents and your youngest sisters, but the home where you grew up, and contact with the rest of your family."

"And now you've lost Mitch," Mrs. Curran added softly, "and Helen's lost Cole."

Robert scowled.

"I know you didn't like him," Mr. Curran said. "And for very good reasons. But it's *still* another loss for your sister."

Robert squinted at the counter. It certainly hadn't occurred to him to see Cole's arrest in that light.

"Not to mention the shock and fear that went with it." Mrs. Curran's eyes shimmered. "That your sister's still *standing* is a tribute to her determination and her courage."

Robert swallowed hard.

Mr. Curran cleared his throat. "We . . ." He hesitated, shook his head, and turned to his wife.

"The decision has to be yours," she said simply. "Yours and Helen's."

"We have to stay together," Robert blurted out. "We *have* to!"

"We know that," Mrs. Curran assured him. "You were apart for far too long as it was."

"And we want *both* of you to come with us . . ." Mr. Curran faltered, took a deep breath, and started again. "But if you decide not to, we want you to know that there won't be any hard feelings. We'll still care about you, and we'll still be there if you ever need us."

"Thank you."

"NOBODY EVER SAID THAT TO US BEFORE." HELEN EMERGED FROM the living room looking rumpled and confused.

"You were listening?" Robert asked.

She nodded and turned toward the Currans. Their expressions rapidly moved from surprise to uncertainty to a wary hopefulness.

"Why?" Helen finally said. "Why're you offering to take us in?"

"You know," Mrs. Curran said slowly, "how things sometimes happen that don't make any sense?"

Helen tipped her head to one side.

"Like your losing your sisters? And our losing Mitch?"

Helen's eyes remained unfocused, but she nodded.

"A lot of life is like that." Mrs. Curran looked down at her hands. "But sometimes, things come together. Like your bringing Robert here to live with you, and his becoming the friend that Mitch so desperately needed."

Helen's forehead became furrowed.

"And now our moving to a house with more space than we'll ever use, and your needing a new place to live." Mrs. Curran looked up and waited until Helen met her gaze. "I've grown terribly, terribly fond of your brother, Helen. And David and I have nothing but respect for the way that you've managed." She looked at Robert and back to Helen. "We'd very much like to have the two of you in our lives."

"We truly would." Mr. Curran said. "In fact, we'd like nothing better than to take you home with us right now."

Helen turned to look at her brother. Deep in her eyes Robert saw the sorrow, the exhaustion, and the worry she had always kept hidden from him. He waited silently, watching the rippling in her throat reflect her inner turmoil.

Helen's breathing began to slow and she closed her eyes. When she finally opened them, she offered Robert a small smile.

"I can be packed in ten minutes. How long do you need?"

Robert crossed the room in three strides, wrapped his arms around her, and squeezed with all his might. "Thank you, *thank* you!"

When he finally released her, Helen took a breathless step backward. "Lord, Runt!" Her eyes grew wide. "Where on earth did you learn to *hug* like that?"

Robert burst into laughter. *"Mitch* taught me!"

The Currans began to laugh, too.

Helen smiled and then shook her head. "I'm not sure I'm up to knowing what else you learned from Mitch."

"Yes you are!" Robert assured her. "You're up to knowing it *all!*"

V. M. Caldwell taught science for fifteen years. The mother of two adopted children, she wrote her first novel, *The Ocean Within,* as an exercise in empathy while waiting for her second son to arrive from India. She lives in upstate New York.

If you enjoyed this book, you'll also want to read these other Milkweed novels.

To order books or for more information, contact Milkweed at (800) 520-6455 or visit our Web site (www.milkweed.org).

The $66 Summer
John Armistead

Milkweed Prize for Children's Literature
New York Public Library Best Books of the Year: "Books for the Teen Age"

A story of interracial friendships in the segregation-era South.

The Return of Gabriel
John Armistead

A story of Freedom Summer.

The Ocean Within
V. M. Caldwell

Milkweed Prize for Children's Literature

Focuses on an older child adopted into a large, extended family.

Tides
V. M. Caldwell

The sequel to *The Ocean Within,* this book deals with the troubles of older cousins.

Alligator Crossing
Marjory Stoneman Douglas

Features the wildlife of the Everglades just before it was declared a national park.

Perfect
Natasha Friend

Milkweed Prize for Children's Literature

A thirteen-year-old girl struggles with bulimia after her father dies.

Parents Wanted
George Harrar

Milkweed Prize for Children's Literature

Focuses on the adoption of a boy with ADD

The Trouble with Jeremy Chance
George Harrar

Bank Street College Best Children's Books of the Year

Father-son conflict during the final days of World War I.

No Place
Kay Haugaard

Based on a true story of Latino youth who create an inner-city park.

The Monkey Thief
Aileen Kilgore Henderson

New York Public Library Best Books of the
Year: "Books for the Teen Age"

A twelve-year-old boy is sent to live with his
uncle in a Costa Rican rain forest.

Hard Times for Jake Smith
Aileen Kilgore Henderson

A girl searches for her family in the Depression-
era South.

The Summer of the Bonepile Monster
Aileen Kilgore Henderson

Milkweed Prize for Children's Literature

A brother and sister spend the summer with
their great-grandmother in the South.

Treasure of Panther Peak
Aileen Kilgore Henderson

New York Public Library Best Books of the
Year: "Books for the Teen Age"

A twelve-year-old girl adjusts to her new life in
Big Bend National Park.

I Am Lavina Cumming
Susan Lowell

Mountains & Plains Booksellers Association Award

This lively story culminates with the 1906 San Francisco earthquake.

The Boy with Paper Wings
Susan Lowell

This story about a feverish boy's imagined battles includes paper-folding instructions.

The Secret of the Ruby Ring
Yvonne MacGrory

A blend of time travel and historical fiction set in 1885 Ireland.

Emma and the Ruby Ring
Yvonne MacGrory

A tale of time travel to nineteenth-century Ireland.

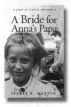

A Bride for Anna's Papa
Isabel R. Marvin

Milkweed Prize for Children's Literature

Life on Minnesota's Iron Range in the early 1900s.

Minnie
Annie M. G. Schmidt

A cat turns into a woman and helps a hapless
newspaperman.

A Small Boat at the Bottom of the Sea
John Thomson

Donovan's summer with his ailing aunt and
mysterious uncle on the Puget Sound tests
his convictions when he suspects his uncle is
involved with shady characters.

The Dog with Golden Eyes
Frances Wilbur

Milkweed Prize for Children's Literature

A young girl's dream of owning a dog comes
true, but it may be more than she's bargained for.

Behind the Bedroom Wall
Laura E. Williams

Milkweed Prize for Children's Literature
Jane Addams Peace Award Honor Book

Tells a story of the Holocaust through the eyes
of a young girl.

The Spider's Web
Laura E. Williams

A young girl in a neo-Nazi group sets off a chain of events when she's befriended by an old German woman.

Stories from Where We Live Series
Edited by Sara St. Antoine

Literary field guides to the places we call home.

The California Coast
The Great Lakes
The Great North American Prairie
The Gulf Coast
The North Atlantic Coast
The South Atlantic Coast and Piedmont

MILKWEED EDITIONS

Founded in 1979, Milkweed Editions is the largest independent, nonprofit literary publisher in the United States. Milkweed publishes with the intention of making a humane impact on society, in the belief that good writing can transform the human heart and spirit. Within this mission, Milkweed publishes in five areas: fiction, nonfiction, poetry, children's literature for middle-grade readers, and the World As Home—books about our relationship with the natural world.

JOIN US

Milkweed depends on the generosity of foundations and individuals like you, in addition to the sales of its books. In an increasingly consolidated and bottom-line-driven publishing world, your support allows us to select and publish books on the basis of their literary quality and the depth of their message. Please visit our Web site (www.milkweed.org) or contact us at (800) 520-6455 to learn more about our donor program.

Interior design and composition by Dorie McClelland
Typeset in Adobe Garamond Pro
Printed on Rolland Enviro 100 paper
by Friesens Corporation.